OUTLAW BUNCH

OUTLAW BUNCH

by
Logan Stuart

Dales Large Print Books
Long Preston, North Yorkshire,
England.

LT ·

34705450 2

British Library Cataloguing in Publication Data.

Stuart, Logan
    Outlaw bunch.

    A catalogue record for this book is
    available from the British Library

    ISBN 1-85389-988-7 pbk

First published in Great Britain by The Western Book
Club, 1960

Copyright © 1960 by Logan Stuart

Cover illustration © Longaron by arrangement with Norma
Editorial S.A.

The moral right of the author has been asserted

Published in Large Print 2000 by arrangement with Roxy
Bellamy

Dales Large Print is an imprint of
Library Magna Books Ltd.
Printed and bound in Great Britain by
T.J. International Ltd., Cornwall, PL28 8RW.

CONTENTS

CONTENTS

CHAPTER ONE

Chance Meeting

It was damnably hot. The kind of heat that made a man pour with sweat and then left him dry as though every particle of moisture had been wrung from him.

The sun burned down and the faintly stirring wind was hot and dry and Frank Sutter cursed roundly as he realized that he had missed the fork road to Brownfield, long back.

He sat the tall chestnut gelding easily, despite his big frame, and through the heat and discomfort and the cursing, his wide mouth curved in a smile. He could cuss himself out and still smile, for Sutter was a big, easy-going, smooth actioned man, who took adversity in his stride, believing, in an odd, pagan-like way, that there was nearly always a reason for everything; even such a small thing as missing the road on a dam' hot afternoon.

Sutter could not have explained his simple code so lucidly. It was something he felt, rather than thought about, anyway an outlaw had little time for fancy words.

He kneed the horse forward to where an overhang afforded both beast and rider reasonable good shade. It was just as hot, but the sun did not burn the skin dry like in the open.

The big man pushed back his weathered, wide-brimmed hat, cocked a booted foot over the saddle horn and built himself a quirly. Yet all the time, his frank blue eyes were darting every which way. His constant glance was on brush and trees fringing the roadside and he even studied his back trail without appearing to be doing anything other than idling away a few loose moments.

Frank Sutter was not scared. Even if there had been a sheriff's posse behind him, he would not be scared; it was not in him. But there *were* three pieces of lead in him; Federal lead which he had received in the last year of the war when riding with Maury's Raiders. And if Frank Sutter and his brothers hated anything at all, it was the Federals ...

Some few yards beyond the tree under which Sutter rested, the brush- and grass-covered verge dipped sharply. He could see, by moving his position slightly, that a shallow basin lay beyond and that the weaving sea of alfalfa was not grass at all, but corn.

He stubbed the quirly out on his smooth-worn saddle horn and edged the gelding forward through the brush.

The sudden glimpse of the single-storied farm house and its run-down barns caused Sutter to wonder momentarily whether this goddam Texas heat was playing tricks on him. Then his easy-going face relaxed and the wide mouth parted in a grin. Why shouldn't there be a farm around here? he asked himself. This was farming land and Brownfield, a farming and cattle town, was but a dozen or so miles distant.

He examined the loads in the two .36 Navy Colts guns that he carried at his hips and, satisfied, thrust the weapons back into their tied down holsters.

He lifted the reins and put his mount to the down gradient, taking care to ride around the cornfield so as not to damage the ripening ears.

He thought maybe that some oldster lived here, judging by the buildings, and he thought of the luke-warm water in the canteen on his saddle and the dipper and pitcher of cool water which, rightly, should be standing in the coolest and shadiest part of the porch yonder.

He had almost reached the house, when his eye caught a blur of movement at the door of the barn.

Unhurriedly, Sutter dismounted while his mind probed the possibility of danger. The Civil War had been over now for sixteen months, yet it was not forgotten. Hatred, enmity and the desire for revenge still sparked off trouble between Yankees and Southerners.

Was he getting spooky, all of a sudden? Sutter considered, and again that slow smile spread to dispel such dark suspicions and he moved like a big cat, quick and silent across the littered yard, and hauled up at the barn door and listened carefully.

He heard the faintest scuffle come from the far corner and a horse nickered and scraped its hooves on the straw-littered board floor.

Frank slowly cocked the gun he had drawn and peered into the sweet-smelling interior. His blue gaze flickered beyond the two draught horses, on to the furthermost corner where a slim figure crouched, holding a pitch-fork in an attitude, half fearful, half defiant.

Sutter walked through the doorway, smiling with a deep down amusement. He eased the hammer back into position and holstered his gun. He said, in a richly pleasant voice: 'Come on, now, lad. I ain't intendin' you any harm. Is this the way you greet thirsty travellers now?'

The slim figure straightened slowly, moving hesitantly step by step, but still keeping those wide eyes fixed to the stranger's face.

'By God!' Sutter exclaimed, astonished

beyond measure. 'Why in hades didn't you say you was a girl? Supposin' I'd plugged you?'

'I—I didn't know what you wanted, or who you were. My gun's in the house. There wasn't much else I could do.'

'You still don't know what I want, do you?' He laughed uproariously as his own simple humour, as though he knew all along he was no great shakes at clever talk. Yet there was something so infectious about this big man and his bellowing laugh that the girl caught some of it and moved forward again and planted herself before him, about six paces away.

Now that she stood in the sunlight which slanted through the open door, Sutter caught his breath. She was young enough in all truth, but the open necked shirt she wore and the tight denim pants clearly showed a ripeness of figure which he had not anticipated.

She flushed before his close appraisal and sought refuge in a kind of pseudo-toughness.

She said harshly: 'What *do* you want,

14

Mister, and who are you? If you're lookin' for Buck Weidman, he shore won't be long gettin' back.'

The outlaw laughed. 'I'm Frank Sutter, if that means anything to you!'

'*Sutter?* Frank Sutter? Not the outlaw bunch—?'

'You heard of us, then?' The big man seemed only coolly surprised.

'Heard of you? Who hasn't? Didn't the Sutter boys ride with some guerrilla outfit an' keep them dam' Feds on the run? And weren't they offered an amnesty or such like an' refused to come in?'

The outlaw smiled. 'Your history ain't bad, Texas, but mebbe what you don't know is, we-all came in—leastways most of us did—but the low-down Blue-bellies fixed an ambush for us. Their word never did mean a darn! So what was we to do but fight and make a run for it?'

'And ever since then you've been on the run?'

Sutter grinned widely. 'Reckon it's them Feds as is on the run when me and the boys are ridin'. Us? We don't haveta worry

15

none, 'cept now and then when things get a mite hot—like this Texas weather—an' we drift down through Missoura an' lay low a while, like now for instance.'

She smiled and laid both her hands on his arms and she was completely unafraid of this man who could break her in two with one hand.

'I'd like to hear some more, Frank,' she whispered, 'but right now I guess you could use a cool drink huh?'

'That's what I came for,' he laughed. 'Reckon I never figgered on findin' such a looker as you, though, when all I wanted was a long drink of water!'

It took six dippers full of water to satisfy Frank's thirst, and when he had finished he smiled and wiped his mouth, squatting down beside the girl on the dusty board floor of the porch.

'You shore had a thirst on you!'

He nodded. 'Reckon that's just about the bestest water I tasted since hittin' this country. Now! How 'bout tellin' me a few things, Texas!'

16

'Such as?'

'Wal, now, yore name, mebbe, an' who works this land an' what's a pretty girl like you doin' with scars across her shoulders?'

For a moment she was too utterly taken aback to reply. She realized that her open-necked shirt had slipped over one shoulder and that Frank Sutter's blue eyes had quickly spotted the whip marks, even though they were old by a month or more. Those across her back were fresh enough to be smarting still like hell-and-be-merry.

It was some moments before she replied and then the words came tumbling from her lips in full flood.

'I'm Etta Storm and my uncle, Buck Weidman, owns this section an' he's a brute! Folks don't know it, though, 'cause he's a kinda two-headed coin and most generally only shows the best side in front of others.

'Then there's Cass. He's Buck's son, which makes him my cousin. He can be mean and ornery at times, but not like Buck. If Buck knew I was a settin' talkin' to a stranger—'

'Where's he at now?'

'You mean the old man? Why, he's over to Brownfield buyin' a new plough share or somethin'. Likely enough he'll be home after dark so's no-one'll see he's mean drunk!'

'And Cass?'

She pushed the long black hair away from her angular face and pouted her full lips.

''Tisn't often they leave me alone, the both of them together, but Cass had to ride in to Mesquite for a horse sale. He's bringin' back a new saddler.' Her mouth twisted and her green eyes narrowed until Sutter could see little more than the thick curtain of her lashes.

Frank built up a quirly, lighted it and regarded her seriously through the blue-grey tobacco smoke. He said: 'Reckon it wouldn't do you much good runnin' away, would it?'

She got up and leaned back against one of the ramada's uprights. 'Do you think I haven't considered such a thing, day and night, for as long as I can remember?'

18

'Sure you have,' Frank answered mildly. 'And any girl or woman alone in the West is goin' to be tagged pretty dam' quick! There's no greys in some folk's minds, only blacks and whites.'

She nodded slowly. 'If—if I only had someone to help me—'

He was on his feet and standing close to her, so fast it seemed impossible. He stood looking down at her, drinking in the almost primitive beauty of this young girl.

'Mebbe something could be done about it, Etta. What say we go back to the barn where the hay is soft and sweet-scented and talk about it?'

She returned his gaze steadily, and in her wide-open eyes was an understanding that brought a madder tinge to the tanned skin of her high cheek bones.

She stood quite still for a long moment, considering the implications of this thing and the alternatives open to her. She could find no alternatives and she swung away from the porch and walked slowly towards the barn, hearing the jingle of Sutter's spurs as he followed her inside and up the short ladder to the hay loft.

Etta lay back, finding it difficult to control the sudden trembling in her limbs. She kept her eyes averted from Sutter's face and found that she was staring fixedly at the big Colts guns in their tied-down holsters.

Frank pulled his glance away from her with a dragging reluctance. Then he laughed so loud that the farm horses skeetered nervously on their halter ropes.

'I was just thinking what Jesse and my brothers'd say if they knew I was with a lovely young filly, 'stead of tending to some chores in Brownfield!'

Etta sat upright. She did not know whether to feel hurt or relieved.

'Brownfield? Then if you should be there, how come—?'

'I musta missed the fork way back,' Frank grinned. 'Found myself on this dirt road which led to a farm and to a girl called Etta Storm! Strange, isn't it, way things work out?'

She could see nothing strange beyond the fact that Frank had happened to ride in, the one time in a thousand, when Buck and Cass were both away for the day.

'You said you was goin' to talk about helpin' me, Frank.'

'Sure I did.'

He took her in his arms. She could not have resisted, whatever. He was as strong as a bull, yet strangely, when he kissed her, it was with less savagery than she had expected.

'Reckon that's about the first time you bin kissed, Etta, huh?'

She was angry this time, but she took care not to show it. This man seemed to sense her moods and the conflicts in her mind. He brought her to the very pinnacle and then, almost laughingly, drew her back.

When she finally summoned up the courage to look at him, he was building a smoke, and his good-humoured face was set in a repose that seemed to reach out and touch her.

She could not help studying him seeing the tanned, muscular chest beneath the kerchief and open shirt. She watched the

21

play of muscles in his neck as he moved his head and she watched the strong, sun-burned hands and the thought came to her that he must have known many women, attractive and desirable.

A fire burned in Etta then, and she took the completed quirly from him and threw it down and leaned forward and gripped his arms and laid her lips on his hard mouth and all thought of Buck and Cass and the farm ran out of her as in a changing dream ...

She felt him move and gently shove her to one side and then he was down the ladder and standing still and alert inside the furled back door.

She brushed the wild hair from her face and only then heard the crunch of wheels across the yard. She recognized the sound of Buck's wagon and, scared now, clambered down the ladder and stood in Frank's black shadow and shivered.

'That the old bastard?' Sutter said softly; and now his eyes were cool and his face no longer easy and good-humoured.

'Yes. But—please, Frank, don't do

anything—don't tell him—'

'You stay in here like you was doin' some chores. Don't worry about Buck or me.'

He eased himself out into the sunlight and began walking towards his horse by the porch as Buck Weidman swung his wagon and team, seeing Frank for the first time.

They stared at each other for a long while, but it was Weidman who dropped his gaze first as he made to fumble with the ribbons, looping them around the whipstock.

'Who are you, Mister?' he asked.

Frank was smiling again now as he considered the man on the wagon seat. He was wearing shabby black and an ancient and battered stetson. His face was narrow and sharp; his eyes dancing and brightly distrustful. He wore a spade beard though the upper lip was shaven.

Weidman looked around uncertainly and his gaze shuttled across to the open barn.

'You lookin' for Etta?' Frank smiled. 'She's right inside doin' her chores.'

'I—I wasn't—I mean that isn't what I

said, stranger. Reckon a man wants to know who he's entertaining, don't he?'

'Sure.' Sutter drew his right hand gun slowly; spun the cylinder and drew back the hammer to its full extent. He glanced up at Weidman, seeing the man's face turn a sickly ashen colour. It reminded Frank of wet putty with a blob of black paint at the bottom.

'Reckon you're right, Mr Weidman. A man never can be too careful over visitors. Say, which side did you favour in the war?'

'I—' Weidman wiped the sweat from his brow with a slow and careful movement of his left hand. 'I—well, this *is* Texas, Mister. You must know how most all of us Texans felt?'

'What you mean is, you helped the Confederacy and skinned every dam' Fed you could lay hands on?'

Weidman's gaze held to the long, blue-black Colt in the stranger's hand with a horrible fascination.

He said thickly: 'I—well, I couldn't fight, but I—that is, me and my son, Cass, did what we could for the Confederacy.'

There! It was out now and Weidman held himself rigid, scarcely daring to breathe; praying that he had made the right choice.

The outlaw grinned: 'Guess that puts us both on the same side of the fence, then. Only difference is, I reckon, I killed mebbe a score o' them bastard Blue-coats!'

Weidman let go his breath in a shivering gasp of relief. Despite the heat, he felt cold. He knew that he had escaped probable death by nothing more than the figurative tossing of a coin or the turn of a card.

Whatever else Weidman was, he was capable of distinguishing between a clod-hopper and a man who would likely kill at the drop of a hat, and the big, smiling man in the yard did not fall into the former category.

Frank's eye fell on a can some thirty yards distant and in the sudden silence of that hot afternoon the metallic click of the Colt's hammer was clearly audible.

For a freezing second of time, Buck Weidman thought he had made his last mistake. Then the air was split by the crash of the gun and lead ploughed a furrow in the hard-baked earth, inches from the can.

A second shot rang out and this time the can leaped several feet as it was squarely struck by the slug from Sutter's gun.

Weidman wrenched his head around and stared at the can and then shuttled his quick, fearful gaze back to the big man.

Etta came to the door of the barn and began running across the yard, her face scared and pale and her eyes clouded with a dark uncertainty.

Sutter was coolly ejecting the spent shells and re-loading. He said, without bothering to glance up: 'It's all right, kid. Just a leetle target practice is all.'

With a supreme effort, Buck Weidman took a tight hold on himself and climbed down from the wagon. In any case, now that Etta was here he felt much safer and then the vague realization that he was in some indefinable way morally dependent upon this miserable girl, kindled inside him a bitter anger.

He said: 'See to the horses, Etta. After that you can unload the wagon.'

Dumbly the girl climbed on to the wagon seat and tooled the vehicle towards the barns.

Frank said drily: 'You got a good helper there, Weidman.'

'Sure.'

Frank moved across to his horse standing hip shot at the porch. He led the animal over to a drinking trough set against the house. He heard Weidman's approach but did not bother to look up. He seemed more concerned that his horse did not over-fill its belly with water.

He said, matter-of-factly: 'I'm Frank Sutter,' and waited for the reaction.

But Weidman had regained a good deal of his nerve. 'I've heard of you and your brothers of course. You did some good work during the war, Mr Sutter, and it's a pleasure to meet you.'

Frank looked up and smiled. 'Mebbe we'll be staying in Texas a while,' he said. 'Mebbe I'll be riding by some more.'

'Any time. Any time. What about a

27

drink right now before you go?'

The outlaw moved his head. 'Reckon I'd best be riding on.' He tightened the surcingle buckle under the saddle, tested it and climbed aboard.

'You know Marshal Calvin at Brownfield?'

'Sure, Mr Sutter. The marshal's a friend of mine. We's all Southerners down here.'

Frank nodded. 'Good. Then that makes us all pals. Be seein' you.'

He lifted the reins and lightly touched the animal's belly with his spurs and rode from the yard and found the narrow track which circumvented the cornfield.

For the space of five or six minutes, Buck Weidman stood as still as a statue, watching the outlaw's big figure eventually recede and disappear into the brush along the road.

He wiped the sweat from his hands and neck with a soiled bandanna. Then he turned on his heel and strode towards the wagon shed.

Etta had already unloaded the plough share and the stores which Buck had brought in and Weidman could hear her working in the stable.

He reached up to the wagon seat and took the whip from its socket and made his way to the stable, treading silently so as to give the girl an even greater scare.

When he came through the doorway, he saw her standing flat against the further wall and all the beauty had gone from her face, leaving it tightly drawn and bereft of expression. Only her eyes reflected any emotion, and fear and hatred swam in their dark blue depths ...

CHAPTER TWO

Outlaw Bunch

It was late in the afternoon when Frank Sutter picked his way through a tangle of underbrush and cottonwoods bordering a small creek.

He put the gelding to the shallow water

and reined in as a man stepped from behind a pile of rocks. This was Jim Sutter, clean-shaven except for black sideburns, and carrying a Henry rifle.

'Howdy, Frank. You get that ammunition alright?'

'Nope. Found me a right pretty filly, though. Guess I'll haveta ride to Brownfield tomorrow.'

Jim Sutter grinned at his brother. It was always the same with Frank. He always managed to find a lady to charm. Yet, be it said, not once had Frank ever allowed such considerations to interfere with their plans.

'Any news, Jim?'

'Lonny's back. Told us he's fixed to buy two hun'ed head of beef. They'll be ready fer us to pick up at Mesquite before the week is out.'

'Good. See you later, Jim.'

Frank rode on and over the slight ridge ahead. There it was, right in front of him! The ranch which they had bought and were going to stock as a front to their other activities!

Maybe they would even make the place pay, he thought, and the idea brought a smile to his dust-covered mouth.

He off-saddled at the corral, turning the gelding into the small enclosure. Then he forked some hay from the nearby barn and pitched it over into the pole corral.

Afterwards Frank moved around to the side of the house, pumped water into a bowl and washed sweat and alkali dust from his face and upper body.

Not until all this had been done in typical leisurely fashion did Sutter mount the porch steps and enter the ranch house.

In the big, litter-strewn living room, he found Lonny, Jesse Lindquist, Bill Hawkes, Cal Selwyn and Brad Keiler.

'Howdy,' he greeted. 'Where the others?'

Jesse said through his beard: 'Over to Mesquite, sampling the town's rye. But don't worry, Doc's with 'em.'

Keiler said: 'Likely they'll all be back afore dusk, Frank.'

Sutter nodded and then asked: 'When does Jim get to bein' relieved?'

'I'm due to spell him come dark, Frank,' Cal Selwyn replied. 'Meanwhile I'd best see about gettin' some grub ready.'

Shortly, the sound of pounding hooves came clear across from the ridge and, looking out, Frank saw Clint Lawler, George Anson and Jack Munroe, headed by Doc Abe Dufresne, riding in.

Later, when they were all seated at the big table, Frank turned to Lonny.

He said: 'Jim tells me you've fixed about the cattle.'

The man who was almost as big as Frank nodded: 'I found a small rancher who figgered on sellin' out an' quittin' the country. Took all his stock; around two hundred head of cattle and six top quality saddlers.'

'How's the money goin', Doc?' Frank asked.

Doc Abe Dufresne passed a notebook across, pointing with a black-nailed finger to several items, including the cattle at five dollars a head.

Frank scarcely glanced at it.

Doc said: 'We got money enough to last

'till you and Lonny and Jesse can build up a front here and in Brownfield.'

'What about Mesquite?'

Dufresne pulled at his goatee beard and shoved his black hat still farther to the back of his grizzled head.

'A tight little Federal community, I'd say, Frank, judging by what me and the boys picked up. If there's any Southerners, which I don't doubt, they're bein' kept mighty quiet by Yankees—'

'Sure. They got the Federal troops quartered nearby,' Clint Lawler snarled.

Frank Sutter leaned back in his chair until it creaked. 'Mebbe,' he said with a slow smile, 'we could do something about that place before we pull out of here.'

'It'd give *me* the greatest pleasure,' Doc Dufresne grunted. 'And I guess that goes for the rest of the boys. How'd you make out in Brownfield, Frank?'

'I didn't. I took a wrong fork and landed up at a farm owned by a yellow-bellied scallawag that claimed he was for the South.'

33

'Bet there was a girl there someplace,' Lonny grinned.

'Sure. A good-looker, too, an' treated worse'n a hard-case nigger. As to Brownfield, I figger on ridin' in soon as we've eaten ...'

It was Jim, the dark, lean one of the Sutter boys, who rode into Brownfield with Frank.

'You go see this Shiro Calvin character, Frank,' he had said, 'while I tend to the purchase of shells.'

Frank had grinned. 'Have it yore way, Jim,' he had said; and guided by the glitter of stars and the brilliant moon they had made Brownfield easily by mid-evening.

Jim rode on down Main in his search for a hardware store still open. Frank, wondering where he would begin, pushed back his hat and found his gaze on a sign that read: 'Shiro Calvin: Marshal's Office & Jail'.

Frank climbed down, tied a rein to the hitching rack and stepped unhindered into the office.

'You the marshal here?'

34

'Sure am. What can I do for you, stranger?'

The man was not so big as Frank, but well-built, nevertheless. He wore a dark hat, vest and boots and a grey woollen shirt. His tanned face was partially hidden by a carefully trimmed brown moustache and imperial.

'Your accent,' Frank Sutter drawled, 'tells me you bin livin' in the South for quite a spell.'

'And yours,' Calvin said, straight and to the point, 'tells me you bin livin' in Missoura, mebbe even Kansas. An' if there's one thing I don't like, it's a man as speaks with a Kansas accent.'

Frank grinned. Already he had noted the picture of Lee pinned to the wall over the marshal's desk.

'All Kansans wasn't abolitionists, Mr Calvin. My name's Frank Sutter an' me an' some of the boys fought with Maury and his raiders.'

'Frank Sutter, eh? So you're the hombre who's been giving Yankee Peace Officers so much trouble. Shake, son! You couldn't 've come with better credentials than if you'd brought a letter from Jeb Stuart himself.'

Frank shook hands. 'You rode with Stuart?'

The marshal nodded. 'An' by God, I'd ride again tomorrow if we could only set the clock back. I—but what did you want, Sutter? Anything I can do to help, you only gotta say!'

Frank had hoped for a good reception. He had gone to the trouble of finding out something about Brownfield and Shiro Calvin before he had ridden south with the boys. Yet he had never expected to have the law offered to him on a plate, just like that.

All right! The law now was supposed to be Yankee law with the blessing of Washington. And the war had been over sixteen months or so. But there were still Northerners and Southerners; still Federals and Confederates even though the latter were now civilians. And there were still banks to rob and express companies to hold up—especially Yankee ones, and a man had the right to live and pay back a few scores into the bargain!

'Me and the boys has taken the old Bennet spread,' Frank said, lighting a quirly.

'Ranchers, huh?'

'You might call us that, Marshal.'

Calvin grinned. 'You stick to milkin' the Federals an' their sympathizers, Sutter, I'll give you all the cover you need.'

'I was hopin' you might see it this way. Now Mesquite—'

'Mesquite's the seat of Jackson County, Sutter, and the sheriff's a Yankee if ever there was one. But don't think they ain't tough. Why, they got several companies of Blue-coats billeted nearby.'

'Yeah. I heard that. Say, what d'you know of a jasper name o' Buck Weidman?'

Calvin scowled and tugged at the waxed ends of his moustache. 'Weidman, huh? Why d'you ask?'

Frank shrugged. 'I met him today. Cain't say I took a shine to him. It's just as well to know who yore friends are, I reckon.'

Shiro Calvin nodded. 'Reckon Buck

Weidman's nobody's friend, 'ceptin' his own. He's got a son called Cass an' a niece name o' Etta. Gossip says he treat the girl real bad.'

'I can vouch for that. There was whip marks on her shoulders.'

Calvin's eyes widened. 'You must've bowled her over real fast, Sutter—'

'Mebbe.' Frank seemed disinterested at the moment and Calvin was smart enough not to press him. This outlaw hombre was big for a start off and the two guns he wore tied down were patently not for ornament.

'You said a while back, Marshal, you'd cover us. How far does this go, you bein' a lawman an' all?'

'If there was any trouble here in Brownfield, I'd have to take action; you know that. But like I said, I got no love for Federal Peace Officers. What you plannin' to do? Live here, frontin' as ranchers?'

Frank nodded: 'Mebbe we'll be here quite a spell at that. What's more, I guarantee we won't get under yore feet, Marshal ...'

Frank found his brother waiting for him on the boardwalk outside Calvin's office.

'You get the ammunition, Jim?'

Jim Sutter nodded towards his horse, tied next to Frank's at the hitching rail. 'In the saddle-bags and the bed-roll. Enough for a small war. How'd you make out with the law?'

'On our side, Jim. But we don't touch this town or anyone connected with it. Calvin's all right; rode with Jeb Stuart. But Mesquite! Wal, now. There's a wide open Yankee town that's gonna be mighty sore before long!'

Jim Sutter grinned. 'How's about a drink afore we ride back?' He pointed across the street to the Golden Slipper and the two ex-guerrilla fighters made their leisurely way across to the saloon.

For a long time, Etta lay on the straw where Buck Weidman had left her clenching her hands until the nails dug into the flesh of her palms.

The humiliation, the bitter hatred that she felt for her sadistic uncle burned more deeply than the pain from the whip lashes across her back.

At first she only felt; without thought, like a dumb and wounded animal. The tears of physical and emotional hurt filled her dark blue eyes and ran unchecked down her dusty face. Her whole body trembled, outraged by the bitterly unjust treatment meted out to it. Slowly she brought her mind as well as her feelings to bear upon her situation.

Not only was there the vicious Buck to have to deal with; there was also Cousin Cass; cunning, cruel and almost as vicious as Weidman himself. But there were differences between father and son. Cass was not a hypocrite. He did not pretend to be one thing and act and speak in the opposite way. Almost did he seem to take pleasure in holding his sins and his bad habits aloft for all to see.

There was another vital difference between the two of them. Cass's silence at times, even his co-operation, could be bought—at a price.

Etta pushed back her lustrous hair and

eased her aching muscles, recalling that first time when Buck had been absent and Cass had tried to make forceful love to her.

Her red lips curved at the memory of the look on his face when for the first time, he realized that Etta was as strong as he was. That she could fight and kick and tear and scratch and that within that shapely figure there had developed an almost unbelievable rawhide strength.

But there had been a far deeper issue that day, a year back, than the mere matching of physical strength. For perhaps the first time Etta had realized that she possessed a weapon not only with which to fight, but with which she could bargain and even dictate terms ...

She turned her tear-streaked face towards the door at the sound of footsteps. She knew it was Cass and she lay there, staring at the open door; continuing to stare long after he had entered and stood lounging against a post.

'So the old man's bin treatin' you like a stubborn mule again?'

Cass, good-looking in a coarse, lusty way, hooked his thumbs in the belt around his denims.

He had long, fair hair and, surprisingly, a roan complexion. He was slight of built—not much taller or broader than Etta—and the knowledge was a worrisome thing that nagged constantly and did nothing to narrow his natural vicious streak.

Etta returned stare for stare, not troubling to mask the coldness in her eyes. No longer did Cass dare to go carrying tales to Buck; not since that day a year back.

She said in a flat voice: 'You gotta cover me, Cass. Get the pistol from my room and bring it here. I must have some more target practice.'

Cass rolled up a quirly and lit it. 'What's all this gun practice? Etty, you fixin' to kill the old man; mebbe me as well?'

'I'm not fixin' to kill anyone, and if I did it wouldn't be you!'

'Why not?' He snapped the question at her like a pistol-shot.

'You've helped me.'

'Sure. But only because you let me make love to you. You don't like me, Etty. In fact I guess you hate me!'

She shook her head. 'Mebbe I do hate you, same as I hate your old man. But you don't get the point. Sure I've paid you, but you've still helped, whether you liked it or not. There's no gettin' away from it!'

Cass Weidman drew on the quirly and exhaled through his broad nostrils. 'What am I supposed to tell Buck this time; you got any ideas? Last time you wanted him outa the way fer nigh on three hours an' I had the devil's own job to cook up a story.'

Etta rose from her position on the straw and walked slowly towards Cass, swinging her hips as she moved.

She put her arms around his neck and placed her mouth on his, feeling the stirring of his body as he breathed more deeply. She closed her eyes, trying to think that this was the big, smiling Frank Sutter and not her own mean-souled cousin.

She had to exert all her strength to draw away from his hungry lips. She said

43

huskily: 'You can think of somethin', Cass. You always do.'

Her words gave him a new and eager confidence. It was several weeks since he had tasted the honey of Etta's lips and he wanted more. It set his brain to working, so that in a very short while he had devised a plan which he thought might work.

As soon as he went up to the house, Etta stepped from the barn and saw the new saddle horse which the boy had brought back from Mesquite.

It was a roan mare and she stood tied to the hitch rail in the lengthening shadows of the barn. Etta thought that it was almost as fine an animal as the one Frank Sutter had ridden. It was broad of chest and long of leg with a beautifully arched neck and a well proportioned body.

The germ of an idea which had lain dormant beneath the surface of Etta's mind now began to grow very slowly. But before she had time to analyse it deeply, Cass was back, a broad smile on his lips and the gun which Etta had stolen from the hardware store in Brownfield tucked

44

into the front of his denims ...

It was not yet dusk when Etta ran down to the lower pasture where Weidman's few cattle grazed. Hurriedly she tore her way through the sheltering brush and trees and on to the small clearing about a mile beyond the house.

Just so long as Weidman remained in the smoke-house, as Cass had promised, he was not likely to hear the shots. In any case, this small grove of cottonwoods, with its tangle of underbrush, tended to deaden sound. Once before when she had been practising, Cass had actually been in the house and he had told afterwards that he had heard no reverberation of shots.

She pinned a playing card to a single tree in the middle of the clearing and faithfully measured out twenty paces.

From her small, precious store of shells, she loaded the .36 Navy Colt and took careful aim. The gun boomed within the confines of this secret spot. Five slugs tore into the edges of the card and for the sixth shot, Etta steadied herself and squeezed the trigger.

When she ran to the tree, she laughed aloud at what she saw. For the very first time she had hit the centre of the card and the realization was like a warming wine running throughout her veins and momentarily obliterating all the unpleasant things of today.

She practised more shots. Then, when the shells were almost gone, she devoted a long time to the mere handling of the empty gun. She hefted it in her hand, judging the balance, getting used to its weight so that her fingers and wrist would grow more than strong enough to throw it around.

The sun was lowering in the west and the faint haze of early dark shimmered over the distant hills and trees as Etta returned to the farm.

She knew that if she could have a little more time she would be as good as most men with a gun and better than some.

She hurried to fulfill her evening chores, taking pails to the pump and carrying them back full to the kitchen.

Buck was talking to Cass over a pile of papers and bills and as she filled water jugs and kettles, a strange atmosphere seemed to lower on the place.

Buck looked at her as though by so doing he could discover whether the whipping he had given her still hurt.

Cass's face wore a loose-lipped grin and when Etta's eyes met his, her cheeks flushed and she turned back to her tasks.

She went out, returning with armfuls of cut wood with which she filled the wood-box by the stove. She turned up the damper and put slices of bacon in a skillet and prepared sauté potatoes with tomatoes and bread ...

Etta was never more thankful than when that meal had been eaten and cleared away and her evening chores completed. She could spend the last few hours of the day in her own tiny room, lying full length on the bunk and thinking, not of the misery of the moment, but of the joy and freedom that was going to be hers so very soon.

47

CHAPTER THREE

Choirboys with Colts

On Sundays Buck Weidman changed his clothes as well as his personality.

He wore a black suit and hat and a shirt which was passably white, thanks to Etta's work at the wash-tub.

This morning, Weidman was feeling generally well disposed, even to Etta. Things were not going too badly now. He had recently added to his small herd of cattle; the corn was high and ripening under the sun and the first harvest of alfalfa had been gathered.

He stood in the yard by the wagon to which Cass had hitched the team, and looked for Etta.

Fearful to keep her uncle waiting overly long, Etta hurried out into the early morning sunshine, dressed in black taffeta

48

and wearing a pale blue bonnet that had belonged to her mother.

To a stranger, she would have appeared quite incongruously dressed; this young girl with the sun-burned face and hands attired in sombre black and with her shining dark hair pinned up under the poke bonnet.

Nor was it easy for Etta to accustom herself to this Sunday apparel after the freedom of shirt, denims and boots.

She climbed to the seat with as much decorum as she was able to muster, while Buck, his spade beard combed and trimmed, began to tool the wagon over the rutted path towards the dirt road.

Sunday was nearly always the highlight of Etta's week. It was usually the only day when she saw other people; when she could, if only for a few brief hours, feel herself a part of the community of Brownfield.

The church service itself meant little or nothing to the girl. Furtively, she would send her glance out from under the shovel-brimmed bonnet, watching the expressions on the faces of the congregation; speculating as to what kinds of lives these men and women led when they were at home; wondering wistfully, sometimes, if they were ever shown love or tenderness, and knowing that this was so when she saw a smoothly contented face.

Although she did not know it, Etta Storm possessed a fine contralto voice; if a trifle immature. During the hymn singing, she let go with such uninhibited abandon that folk nearby would turn their heads with an impalpable smile or nod of approval.

Buck Weidman did not object to this. In a way, it made him feel a more important, more respected member of the community.

But today, Etta's was not the only fine voice raised to reach and echo around the tin roof of the church. Close at hand, three men dressed in immaculate black broadcloth used their rich tenor voices, not only to praise the Lord but also to invite the attention of the women-folk present.

Two of the men were big, the third,

somewhat smaller, and when the fair-haired one turned his head and looked straight into Etta's eyes, her heart missed a beat as she saw that the man was Frank Sutter.

He smiled, recognizing her despite her changed appearance, and as he shifted the hymn book from one hand to the other, Etta glimpsed the smooth-worn black handle of a Colt's gun beneath the broadcloth coat.

How long the preacher droned on, or what he said, Etta had no idea, but at length the congregation was gushing out into the sunlight and splitting into chattering groups.

Etta saw that Buck was talking to such a group of men who, despite their Sunday best, looked like down-trodden nesters. Then, as before, her heart stood still and the colour ran over her high cheeks as Frank, hat in hand, bowed gallantly before her.

'Reckon I never figgered you as a church-goer, Etta. But you sure look good—'

'Come to that, Frank, I never knew

outlaws went to church!'

Her hand flew to her mouth as though she would stop the words that already had escaped, but the big blond man was laughing with such gusto that heads turned and measuring glances were laid first on Frank and then on Weidman's niece.

One or two of the women-folk frowned in open disapproval at sight of the Storm girl talking and laughing with a comparative stranger. Some of the men merely grinned, wishing they were as big and young and as full of vigour as this Frank Sutter hombre, whom rumour had it was a wanted man.

The other two Sutter boys were talking with Shiro Calvin, and if the marshal accepted these newcomers then so did Brownfield, to the last man and woman.

'When you figurin' on riding by again, Frank? I—what I mean is, do you often—?'

Sutter smiled. Etta thought that she had never seen anyone so handsome, what with the sun glistening on his blond hair and touching his tanned face.

'Mebbe I'll ride back with you now. Why not, less'n yore uncle has other ideas!'

Weidman, catching sight of Etta and Frank, broke away from his fellow nesters, a smile parting his thin mouth.

'Did I hear you say you'd be payin' us another visit, Mr Sutter? Well now, anytime you feel like—'

'I feel like it now.' Frank was still grinning, but the smile no longer reached to his blue eyes and, hurriedly, Weidman extended the invitation which this dangerous man had forced upon him.

Buck's laugh sounded brittle and forced. 'What's wrong with now, like you say? Mebbe you'll have a meal with us?'

Frank nodded. 'Sure. You an' Etta go on while I get my horse from the livery.'

The only one who seemed to be under no constraint at the dinner table was the outlaw himself.

Cass looked like a kid whose nose had been put severely out of joint. Weidman, anxious to please, experienced great difficulty in maintaining his rôle of the genial host.

Etta said little, and except for when Sutter spoke to her she seemed lost in some far-off world of her own.

It was galling for Weidman to have to allow Sutter to take Etta for a walk. He cared not for the girl's sake; it was just that he and Cass had to buckle to and do the chores which were Etta's by right of her being fed and clothed and housed by her kinsfolk.

For a moment it almost seemed to Etta that Frank had taken her under his wing.

'What about the dishes, Etta?' Weidman had asked with a sickly smile.

'Sure. I'll do them right away.'

But Frank brushed the idea aside with his easy smile and soft voice. 'Reckon everyone's entitled to one day off a week, Weidman. What d'you say, huh?'

'Why, sure. It's just that—'

'Let Cass do the dishes,' Frank grinned. 'Me an' Etta's goin' for a walk.'

Etta knew, beyond any shadow of doubt, that Buck would take it out of her hide as soon as Frank had gone, yet it was worth it for two reasons.

First, Etta Storm was attracted to this man, whoever he was and whatever he had done. Second, he might well be the means of helping her escape from her prison without bars ...

They lay on the sun-cured grass of the ridge overlooking the farm. The breeze was warm and the sun fierce, but up here a single cottonwood spread its patchwork pattern of welcome shade and for a while they drowsed in the sheer contentment of the moment.

'Those two men in church with you,' Etta said presently. 'They were like you, 'specially the big one.'

'Sure. They're my brothers, Lonny an' Jim. We-all got the old Bennet spread now, Etta. Likely we'll be stayin' around this neck o' the woods for a spell.'

'How can you be so—well, so cool about everythin', Frank? Ain't you scared some Peace Officer's gonna trail you here and—'

Frank rolled over and held Etta's shoulders and kissed her open mouth. He drew away for a moment and said softly: 'We can talk later, Etta ...'

Etta looked up at the sun and judged the time at around four-thirty. *It just shows how scared Buck is of Frank,* she thought, *else he'd bin calling for me long ago.*

She put her sideways glance on Sutter, seeing him relaxed and smoking, his black coat smooth and unruffled, just as though nothing had happened. She could just see the butt of one of his guns which he had buckled on again.

She said softly: 'I see you favour the big .36 Navy Colts, Frank.'

He looked at her in mild surprise.

'You interested in guns, then?'

She nodded. 'I've got one like yours, that's how I know. I practise with it whenever I can.'

He sat upright. 'Don't tell me a kid like you can handle one of these things?'

She looked at him through narrowed eyes, veiled by the thick black lashes.

'A kid?'

'No,' he smiled. 'I guess I can never rightly call you that again, Etta.'

'I'd like to try one of those.'

'Sure.' This time he laughed outright.

56

'Mebbe you'd like to put a slug in me!'

'You can empty it first if you don't trust me!'

'Why should I trust you?'

'You've told me a bit about yourself and the boys; that you're outlaws. Why tell me all this if you don't trust me?'

The outlaw grinned. 'I told Shiro Calvin even more, but you don't see him ridin' over here or to the Bennet spread with a posse, do you?'

'Then that's all the more reason—'

'Nope. They's two different things, Etta. The South is still the South, even if we was licked. Besides which, anythin' I say or 've said could sure be denied dam' quick and no-one could do a thing, even if it came to it.' He shook his head. 'For all I know, you might just wanta kill me for the sheer hell of it or—because you've hated my guts ever since that day in the barn—'

'You know that's not true! Leastways you oughta know.'

He was silent a moment, thinking things out in his careful, methodical way. He had met most kinds of woman, had seen most

57

every kind of action, good and bad, during the war.

Frank Sutter's life and experiences had made him a pretty good judge of people—even women—though he might well have been surprised had anyone told him this.

He stood up and drew both guns. One he held loosely in his right hand; the other he handed to the girl, butt first.

Fifty yards away lay a piece of deadwood. 'Try that, Etta, an' don't forget I could drop you in less'n a second!'

She hefted the gun in her hand, getting the feel and balance of it before she thumbed back the hammer. She said in a tight voice: 'See that black knot where a branch has bin broken?'

Without waiting for a reply, she took aim and loosed off all six shots in a matter of a few seconds.

To Sutter's astonishment, he saw chips of wood fly from all around the tiny target which the girl had selected.

She turned to him with a faint smile, her eyes, in the afternoon sunlight, almost the colour of the gunsmoke that curled upwards from the muzzle of the Navy Colt. Then she handed Frank the empty gun and together they walked over to the deadwood and examined the target.

Five of the six slugs had buried themselves in a rough circle around the dark knot. One slug had ricocheted and ploughed a furrow along the limb itself.

From the house below a shout went up, and as Frank and Etta turned they could see the small, black figure of Buck Weidman gesturing in a frenzy of anxiety.

'Don't tell him I can use a gun, Frank! *It's somethin' he mustn't know!*'

Sutter moved his arm to and fro and shouted back to Weidman.

'It's all right! Just practisin' a few shots, is all!'

Re-assured, Weidman retraced his steps to the house, and Frank turned to the girl, replacing the one gun in its holster and filling his empty one with fresh loads.

'That shootin' was near as durn good as I ever saw,' he said. 'Ain't many of the boys as could beat that, I reckon.'

She stood close to him and raised up her face, giving him the full battery of her wild beauty.

She said huskily: 'I could be useful to you, Frank! Oh, sure; mebbe you've never had a woman ride with you, but what difference does that make. I can look after myself, just so long as I've got a gun and a horse—'

'No dice, Etta. Mebbe you can use and gun and ride, but a girl like you would be—'

'You think your men'd take advantage of me because I'm a woman?' she demanded fiercely. 'I tell you, Frank, they wouldn't dare touch me, and I'd take orders only from you!'

'Yet that little runt Weidman can whip you whenever he's a mind to?'

'You think he'd lay a hand on me if he knew I could shoot him down as easy as fallin' off a log?'

'Then why don't you?' Frank asked simply. 'You said you've got a gun.'

'I tell you I'm gettin' out of here when the time's ripe,' she hissed back. 'You know dam' well I cain't pull up stakes without a horse and without some place to go!'

When they had returned to the shade of the cottonwood, Frank said: 'What about Cass? Seems to me he's ornery enough to spill anything that's likely to get you another lashing.'

Etta said in a low, hard voice: 'I know how to handle Cass.'

It took a moment or two for Sutter to absorb the full significance of the girl's words. It was more the bitter tone of her voice rather than the words themselves which told him what she meant.

'I see. So it's like that, huh?'

'What else d'you think I can do? Sure, I'm stronger than Cass and can hold him off, but there's only one way to stop him carryin' tales—' She broke off abruptly, feeling suddenly wretched about the whole business; about life itself. What had it offered her so far? Nothing much beyond an existence of hard, slaving work and whippings.

She had seen in Frank a rescuer. If not

a knight in shining armour, at least a man, strong and feared, who could lift her easily from this hateful and humiliating slough of despond. But Frank Sutter had turned down her suggestion, almost instinctively and without consideration.

Well! She would show him that she could make herself useful, perhaps invaluable. There were other things besides riding fast and shooting well; things which sometimes only a woman could do, like obtaining vital information, for instance!

Of a sudden, she thought of Oscar Meeks, her uncle's cousin. Oscar Meeks whom none of them here ever saw. Oscar Meeks who worked as an employee of the Bassett Express Company in Mesquite.

For the next few weeks, life went on much as before in its humdrum way for Etta. There were fewer tongue lashings and only one whipping.

Buck was away more often and so long as the work was done he found less fault with his niece than he had done before Frank Sutter showed up.

Etta connected the two things in her mind, grasping their related significance with all the quickness of a more mature woman. Here was another weapon for her to use against Buck. Mebbe he was scared she would set the outlaw on to him.

As for Cass, he, too, worried her less, being increasingly occupied with the cattle which the ambitious Weidman was slowly building up.

One morning Frank rode by and Weidman eagerly released her from her chores in the presence of the big, softly-spoken gunman.

She tackled Frank again about joining the band, but he only laughed and soon silenced her by regaling her with tales of some of their exploits, both during and after the war.

She listened intently, not because she had relinquished her original idea, but because every piece of information gathered and garnered about Frank and his band might stand her in good stead when the time came.

He did not stay so long this time, telling

her that he had business to attend to.

'You mean you're plannin' a raid, Frank?'

He regarded her for a long moment, almost with the stirrings of anger in his blue eyes; then he slowly relaxed. 'You got any ideas in that pretty head o' yours, Etta, you sure better keep them to yourself, else one o' these days you might find yourself squirming on hot lead!'

She caught hold of his arms with a sudden strength that surprised him. 'Cain't you see I'm only tryin' to help you?' she breathed fiercely. 'Supposin', for instance, you wanted an alibi. All I'd haveta say was you were over here at the time! Don't you see what a help—?'

He caught her arms in one hand and gripped them until she thought the bones would break.

'Your first thought right now, Etta, is to quit this place you hate so much, for good an' all. Still, that idea of supplyin' an alibi might not be so bad at that.'

'Then you'll—?'

'I'll think about it,' he told her roughly,

and got up and moved across to his horse and stepped into the saddle and rode away with the barest lift of his arm.

She stood there a long time, in the shadow of the barn, watching him intently, her face dark and savage with the anger that rowelled her like a spur ...

As soon as Frank reached the dirt road, he put the chestnut gelding to a mile-eating lope.

He was beginning to know this country fairly well by now and, by using a series of short cuts which he had discovered, he was able to reach Mesquite soon after noon.

Mesquite, even though a county town, had not been big enough for the carpet-baggers to bother about. Even so, there was marked evidence, wherever a man looked, that this was a Federal stronghold. Yankee names had been borrowed for some of the saloons and dance halls and even a few of the stores. It was not an uncommon sight to see anything from one to a dozen Federal troopers tromping the boardwalks at most times.

Frank spotted Lonny lounging back

against a clapboard wall outside the Lincoln House and immediately rode over.

He stepped from the saddle, tied his horse and exchanged the makings with his brother.

'Where's Jim?'

Lonny said softly: 'Scoutin' round the back to see what he can find out.' He jerked his head in the direction of the bank yonder. 'Looks like a tough nut to crack, Frank. Don't see how we can do it without more information.'

'We'll do it,' Frank replied, confidently. Yet for all his apparent calm, he was beginning to feel a faint unease. Lonny was no fool, nor was he ever afraid, just so long as he had a couple of guns and a good horse under him. Frank minded the time when Lonny had out-fought eight Federal cavalrymen, killing four and putting the others to flight. How the boy had not been cut to ribbons, Frank had never known.

'Go find him,' Frank said, 'and meet me over there in the Yellow Rose.'

Lonny pulled down the brim of his hat

and stepped from the boardwalk, making his unhurried way towards the alley at the side of the bank.

Some fifteen minutes later the three Sutter boys were drinking in the Yellow Rose saloon and quietly discussing the tough job that lay ahead of them ...

CHAPTER FOUR

Clean as a Whistle

'How much longer we gotta sit around here playin' nurse to a bunch of cattle, Frank?'

The men were lounging in a variety of attitudes on the porch of the Bennet ranch house; Frank and his two brothers, Doc Dufresne, Jesse Lindquist, Bill Hawkes, Cal Selwyn and Brad Keiler. Lawler, Anson and Munroe were with the cattle.

There was no armed guard now, down near the creek, for the Sutter gang had been accepted by Brownfield. Within the space of a month or so, they had become respectable ranchers. Everyone knew that Frank Sutter and his 'cowboys' had bought and stocked the old Bennet spread and folk were already referring to it as Sutter's place or the Lazy S, which brand Frank had registered and burned on to his stock.

It was pretty evident that these three fine, upstanding brothers had earned themselves a high reputation from the word go.

No-one in or around Brownfield regarded them as outlaws. They were the victims of circumstances; having been branded as thieves and killers by the abominably unjust Federal laws of Missouri and Kansas at the close of the war.

It was Brad Keiler who had put the question this fine morning and, truth to tell, this enforced inactivity was beginning to pall somewhat.

Sutter looked up and laid his cool blue gaze on Brad.

'I told you-all, this job's a tough nut to crack. It needs a heap of plannin' and that's just what me an' Lonny an' Doc's been doin' this last few days.'

'We put the fear of God into towns bigger'n Mesquite before now, Frank,' Jesse Lindquist murmured.

'That was in the past. Things has changed somewhat since them war days. You all bin into Mesquite now an' you all seen the size of the place and the problems we's up against.

'Sheriff Carter and his deppities is all ex-Union soldiers and they still hate the South with all their guts.'

'What else, Frank?' Keiler grunted.

Sutter said: 'This won't be one o' them raids where we all ride into town yellin' and shootin' and with duster coats for disguise.' He shook his head. 'No. It just wouldn't work. We gotta tackle this job like we was comin' up on a Federal post, and above all we've got to keep open our line of retreat.'

'What's the plan, then?' Selwyn wanted to know. 'Sounds to me like you got somethin' figgered out.'

'We have. Lonny an' Jim an' me has bin over that town in the last few days with a fine tooth comb and we shore picked up some useful knowledge. Tell 'em, Lonny!'

The big dark one, so like Frank and yet so different, ran his eye over the assembled men. He commanded almost as much respect as brother Frank when it came to real serious business such as this.

'First off,' he said shortly, 'this isn't goin' to be a big party. Me, Jim, Frank and Doc, here, will be all. We mosey into town nice an' quiet, about eight-thirty, just before the bank starts gettin' down to the day's business.'

'What about the getaway?' Lindquist asked. 'What about Carter and his deppities?'

Lonny held up his hand. 'Wait for it, Jesse; you ain't heard the half of it yet. We found out that Carter'll be out of town next Monday morning. That's the time we figger best for pullin' this job. If things go the way we've planned, no-one'll know the bank's bin robbed till the first customer shows up!'

'An' if there's a hitch?' Brad Keiler put in.

Frank said, matter-of-factly: 'Then we shoot our way out, like we done a dozen times before. Afterwards we split up an' make our way back here.'

'How 'bout tracks, Frank?' Jesse queried. 'Mebbe this Carter hombre's a good enough tracker to pick up your trail even the next day, mebbe.'

Frank laughed. 'I taken care o' that, too. Now let's go inside an' work the whole thing out with a sketch map. Come on, Jesse, you're in this, too ...'

At around seven o'clock on Monday morning, the three Sutter boys and Doc Dufresne mounted up and left the Lazy S. They rode dark brown horses with no obvious distinguishing marks.

'You reckon Jesse and Clint Lawler can handle their end of it, Frank?' Jim asked.

'Don't be a fool, Kid,' Lonny growled. 'Frank knows what he's doin' else he wouldn't 've picked 'em.'

'Sure.' Jim nodded and swung his mount

in behind the others.

They rode slowly and with care. Every so often, Frank would move on ahead and survey the countryside and the trails they were using. Only once did they have to wait, when a tinker's wagon crossed their trail about a mile ahead. The fewer people who saw them the better, so Doc and the Sutter boys figured. It was a good time to pick, anyway. No-one seemed to be riding the trails and even in Mesquite few people were as yet abroad.

They hit the county seat neither from the north nor the south but made a detour, coming up the alley which led to Main Street and the bank.

The four of them sat their horses in the early morning shadows as cool as all get-out. Some few yards yonder, towards Main Street, lay Burr Parker's livery stables.

Frank nodded towards the livery and then addressed the bigger of his brothers. 'Fix him, Lonny, an' make it good.'

Lonny Sutter slid from his saddle and walked quietly to the partially open stable door.

Frank and the others watched him as he stepped inside and disappeared from view. The seconds ticked by and there was not one of these hard-eyed riders whose heart did not begin to beat a trifle faster as minutes dragged on into what seemed an alarming period of time.

At a signal from Frank they moved up a little until they were almost level with the livery doors.

Lonny suddenly appeared, grinning and waving them in. There were a few horses in the stalls but no sign of the hostler, and Frank's eyebrows lifted at Lonny.

'He's out cold an' trussed tighter 'n a chicken. Where you leavin' the hosses?'

'Right here, by the door. Doc! You see they's ready for us when we need 'em!'

Dufresne nodded and pulled out a silver watch. 'Right on schedule, Frank. It's a little after eight-thirty.'

'All right, Jim,' Frank said. 'You walk up to the street. We'll be waitin' for your signal.'

Jim Sutter's hat was pulled down to

shade his eyes from the sun's oblique rays. He looked like any other cowpoke or range rider with his dark woollen shirt and jacket and his trousers tucked into dusty knee boots; except that ordinary cowpokes didn't usually carry two strapped down guns. That was why Jim's coat was loosely fitting even when it was buttoned across as now.

He stopped at the end of the alley and built himself a smoke and surveyed the street over his cupped hands as he applied the sulphur flame to his cigarette.

Watching carefully, Frank saw Jim's hand go into his coat pocket and re-appear grasping a kerchief.

Immediately, Frank Sutter jerked his head and Lonny fell in beside him as they strode with deceptive speed towards their goal.

They did not pause to converse with Jim but brushed right by him.

They could both see now that store-keepers were sweeping out their premises and displaying goods outside on the boardwalk. A few people were abroad, but no-one was within a hundred yards or so as Frank rapped sharply on the glass panels with a silver dollar.

A minute or so passed before the blind shot up and a bespectacled teller showed behind the door, shaking his head to and fro and mouthing the words that the bank was not yet open.

As though not understanding or perhaps giving an impression of unusual urgency, Frank waved a thousand dollar bill at the owl-faced clerk and rattled the door with the vigour of a norther striking town.

It did the trick, for in a moment the door was unlocked and Frank slid inside followed by Lonny, who had appeared as though from nowhere. As the doors closed behind them, the blinds were pulled down once more. There was nothing to show that Mesquite's bank was about to be robbed.

Inside, the terrified teller moved back uncertainly, his hands above his head, his petrified gaze shuttling from the big Navy Colt's gun to Frank Sutter's cold, unsmiling face.

Lonny's gun was directed on the cashier at the counter.

'Get back against the wall,' Frank told the teller, 'an' mebbe you won't get hurt.'

'Why—you're Mr Sutter, aren't you? I—I've seen you around town, haven't I? Tell me, is this some kind've a joke?' Despite his fear the man was able to get the words out fairly clearly and quickly and that was fatal for both the bank employees.

Sutter had coolly weighed all this up when planning the raid, realizing that if he were to show himself in order to get the bank doors unlocked, then whoever obliged him might have to be killed. Unfortunate, but there was no other way.

Now that the fool had addressed him by name for the cashier to hear, it meant there would have to be two killings.

Frank shoved the scared teller against the wall and buffaloed him with the barrel of his gun. The man's legs went limp and his body slid to the floor as blood began to ooze from his head and trickled down his face.

Lonny, his voice thick and threatening, said: 'All right, Mister, open the safe!'

The cashier was a younger man, somewhere in his mid-forties, and Frank had taken the trouble to find out that he was married and had a son and daughter.

He stood now, scared but resolute, staring first at the unconscious teller and then at the two gunmen before him. He had his nerve, for, pallid as he was, with the sweat shining on his face, he shook his head and found his voice.

'I'm not opening the safe for any bank robbers—'

'Brave words, Mister,' Frank drawled, 'but if it's not open in five seconds, your family's goin' to get it right in the guts!'

The man went an ashen colour, swayed a little and then steadied himself, both hands clearly visible on the counter. 'I'll open it right away,' he croaked, and bent down and fumblingly inserted a key into the door.

From underneath his coat, Lonny produced a wheat sack and proceeded to gather up all the loose currency on the counter. As soon as the safe was open, he kicked the cashier aside and grabbed at the bundles of notes and started stuffing them into the sack.

When the bills had been transferred, he took silver and gold pieces and pokes of gold dust until the wheat sack was fairly bulging.

Frank had moved back to the door and was taking a peek through the curtain. He could see Jim still leaning against a post but the kid's eyes were on the door and his head jerked slightly but quickly as he saw part of Frank's face behind the curtain.

Frank strode back across the room. 'Make it fast, Lonny. We's takin' too much time!'

'I reckon that's about the lot.' Lonny tied the sack and looked at him and Frank nodded and levelled his gun at the cashier crouching on the floor near the safe. Terror made a ghastly mask of his face and every pore on his face, it seemed, held a globule of sweat.

'No—no! You cain't, Mr Sutter! I won't tell—honest to God—!'

His protestations were cut short by the roar of Frank Sutter's gun at close quarters. It only needed the one shot for it was quickly obvious that the cashier was now very dead.

Lonny looked at the oldster lying against the wall. He was showing signs of coming to life. Frank nodded and this time it was Lonny's gun that roared out as a slug was sent crashing into the defenceless body.

Lonny wasn't quite sure, for blood was streaming from high up on the oldster's chest. Lonny reckoned that the heart should be a trifle lower and the safest bet. He aimed again and this time he was satisfied.

The three shots had echoed around the confines of the bank, sounding pretty loud to the Sutter boys, and in a moment they were at the doors, unlocking one of them and waiting for Jim's signal again.

Two men were crossing the street at an angle to the bank and, with a door a fraction open, Frank heard one say, 'Sounded like shots to me, Jim. Seemed to come from somewhere over here.'

'Sounded like to me someone was mebbe usin' blastin' powder.'

Jim Sutter, hat pulled well down, was every inch the idle but helpful onlooker. He stretched out an arm and pointed down-street. 'I heard somethin',' he said. 'Sounded like a gun bein' let off across one o' them vacant lots.'

The men nodded, paused and then proceeded on down-street, with nothing better to do at the moment than to see if the loafer was right.

They didn't turn round, which was as well for them, because Frank and Lonny were by now emerging from the bank.

It was no more than a few steps to the alley and it was doubtful that anyone across the street even noticed them as they disappeared off Main.

But once at the livery they moved faster. Doc was ready and waiting for them, holding the horses. In a matter of seconds, all four men were riding away from Mesquite towards the cottonwood-lined creek a mile or so distant.

Doc said: 'I thought I heard that .36 of yours, Frank.'

Frank said drily: 'You did, but I reckon the citizens of Mesquite ain't sure yet what's happened.'

At the creek, Frank turned to Abe Dufresne: 'You get back, Doc, the way we planned, an' take care to ride in from the south like we always do.'

'Don't you reckon I'd best wait 'till we sight the herd?'

For answer, Frank Sutter pointed to a faint dust-cloud coming in from the north-east some three-four miles from Mesquite.

'There's Jesse now. Right on time!'

Dufresne nodded, neck-reined his horse and began to make a wide circle before approaching Mesquite.

Lonny grinned. The bulging wheat sack was tied across his saddle horn. He said: 'Clean as a whistle, Frank; not even a witness!' He turned in the saddle and clapped an arm on Jim's shoulders. 'You sure put those two fellows off, Jim. For a moment I figgered they was comin' inside the bank.'

Jim laughed. 'Told 'em I thought someone was firing a gun way down the street across to those vacant lots!'

'They didn't get a good look at you?' Frank asked.

'No. My hat was well down. I was watchin' 'em close but they didn't take one good look at me. Funny, ain't it?'

'Come on,' Frank reminded them. 'We gotta herd to meet!'

There were still no sounds of pursuit, so that the Sutter boys could afford to ride at a leisurely gait. Only the bulging wheat sack might be a source of embarrassment if they were unlucky enough to meet anyone now.

But things seemed to be working smoothly enough as they intercepted the herd of some hundred or so beeves and quickly gave Jesse and Cal the news.

There was no time wasted. The bank money was split roughly into two and quickly stashed in the saddle-bags on Jesse's and Cal's ponies.

Straight off, Jesse and Cal took to the brush, while Frank, Lonny and Jim took over the herd, just as though they had been trailing the beef all along.

It was a good alibi and one which was shortly to be put to the test.

Back in Mesquite, deputy Herb Rayner was seated in back of the sheriff's office, reading a month-old newspaper. He heard the three faint-sounding explosions but paid them no never-mind, absorbed as he was in his reading.

When he put the paper down, he sat back in the sheriff's chair and the thought came to him, unbidden, that those muffled sounds *could* have been a gun going off somewhere.

Jake Sepple, the other deputy, was still at breakfast; nevertheless, Rayner walked to the door and stood there a moment in some uncertainty.

The town seemed quiet enough beyond the fact that it was waking up, yet a faint un-ease touched Rayner and nudged him into eventual action.

He locked the door and moved along the boardwalk until he came opposite the bank. He nodded to several townspeople whom he knew who seemed to be doing the normal kind of thing in the normal kind of way.

Any moment now, Herb Rayner thought, the bank will be opening. His gaze was on the two doors; why, he had no idea.

Shortly, he continued on and then pulled up abruptly, remembering that he had seen one of those doors slightly ajar. Only then did the significance strike him. He looked at the clock over the Express Office and saw that it wanted another eight minutes before the bank would be open for business.

It occurred to him then that as a general rule neither Bates nor Townsend unlocked the door until the stroke of nine.

By the time Herb Rayner reached the opposite boardwalk, he found that he was running ...

CHAPTER FIVE

Etta Rides Out

Lonny and Jim were riding point on the small herd, one on either flank. Frank chose for himself the drag position where, despite the rising dust, he had a good view of their back-trail.

They were making slow but easy progress and for about the tenth time in half an hour, Frank twisted round in the saddle and laid his narrowed gaze over the trails that quartered towards Mesquite.

Something back there held him still a moment as he put the battered field glasses to his eyes. Then his dust-caked lips broke into the familiar easy-going smile and he replaced the glasses in his saddle-bag and wheeled his mount around the rear of the herd.

Lonny turned in the saddle with raised

eyebrows as Frank's voice lifted above the dull rumbling drum-beat of the cattle's hooves.

'Posse headin' this way, Lonny. You know what to do!'

With that, he turned and circled back and came up to Jim on the left flank of the herd. The dark, lean youngster was aware by now what was happening.

'You figger they suspect us, Frank?'

The big man grinned. 'Suspect three cowpokes hazin' their own herd to their own ranch? Why should they? As to that, I don't give a goddam if they do. You go on watchin' these critturs, Jim, an' don't let that posse get 'em spooked!'

By the time Herb Rayner and Jake Sepple arrived at the head of some eight or nine armed men, Frank was back pushing the drag and spitting dust.

'Hey, Mister! You seen any riders burnin' leather in the last half-hour or so?' Rayner shouted.

Frank brought his mount to a halt and surveyed the gathered men in well-feigned surprise.

'What's goin' on?' he asked. 'Sure looks like—'

'Never mind what it looks like,' Rayner snarled. 'Jest answer my questions. Say! Haven't I seen you around Mesquite?'

'Likely you have,' the outlaw agreed mildly. He nodded to Lonny and Jim who were keeping the herd moving at a snail's pace. 'Me an' my two brothers there ride into Mesquite now and again—'

'Who are you, then?'

'Why,' Frank replied in a tone of patient explanation, 'we run the Lazy S, east of Brownfield aways. We already got around two hun'ed head and now we're trailin' this herd in.'

'You got a bill of sale?' Sepple asked. 'That brand ain't no Lazy S.'

Frank looked shocked. 'Course it's not Lazy S 'cause we don't usually brand on the trail.' He produced a crumpled bill of sale showing that the cattle had been sold only that day to one Frank Sutter of the Lazy S in Jackson County, Texas. The price was there and the number and also the illegible signature of the original owner.

'Come on, Herb,' one of the men snapped. 'What in bloody hell you tryin' to prove?'

Rayner curbed his frisky horse. He said: 'Sutter? That name sounds kinda familiar—'

'Mebbe you're thinkin' of Sutter's Mill, way back in Californy,' Frank grinned. 'Anyways, you haven't told us what's happened an' why the posse.'

Rayner relaxed a fraction.

'The bank in Mesquite was held up and robbed less'n an hour back—'

'And you're lookin' for the bandits?'

It was difficult to tell whether this man Sutter was mildly simple or was being plain sarcastic. But Rayner nodded. He said: 'Two employees of the bank were shot dead, so we're lookin' not only for robbers, but for cold-blooded killers to boot.'

'Well,' Frank offered, 'you can ask my brothers, of course, but I'm pretty sure we'd seen any riders fannin' the breeze was they around like you said. Truth is, Mr Deppity, we's had our hands full with this herd.'

'They look peaceful enough,' one of the posse men growled.

'Sure. They's gettin' a mite tired now,' Frank said, and added pointedly, 'and so am I.'

'All right,' Rayner said. 'Mebbe we'll look you up sometime, Sutter, an' see what kind've cowhands you an' your brothers are.'

'Do that,' Frank invited, and grinned as the posse men neck-reined their mounts and headed back towards Mesquite.

Etta lay back on her bunk, hands clasped behind her head. Now that she had made her decision, she felt an almost over-riding urge to start. But she schooled herself to some semblance of patience and remained still, listening to the noises of the night and the voices of Cass and Buck filtering through from the kitchen.

It seemed an age before their talk eventually ceased and with heart beating a trifle faster she waited tensely for the familiar sounds of closing doors.

Even then, she had to remain cool and

still and give them time ...

It was nearly two weeks now since Sutter had last ridden by and, quite suddenly, the conviction had come to Etta that Frank was not going to lift a finger to help her. If she were to escape from this hateful household, she would have to do so herself, alone and unaided.

He had never taken her seriously, least of all when she had tried to persuade him that she could be of some use in his activities.

She clenched her teeth together. Well! Maybe Mr Frank Sutter would learn different in the near future! Maybe! If everything went as she had planned it!

Presently, Etta swung her legs over the edge of the bunk and padded across the small room in her bare feet. She shrugged into her coat, clapped a battered hat upon her head and thrust the Navy Colt's gun into the front of her denims.

Lastly she caught up her boots and a wheat sack and blew out the lamp.

She grasped the chair wedged against the door and moved it away. Then she quietly lifted the latch and eased the door open with heart-tripping slowness.

Gently, scarcely daring to breathe, she closed the door and made her soft-footed way to the kitchen.

She opened the cupboard and dropped bread and meat and cheese into the sack and various smaller items of food which she might need.

Then Etta's gaze lifted to the top shelf of the cupboard whereon various tins and jars stood. One of them, she knew, contained a sizeable wad of notes. She had seen Weidman furtively place money at the top of this cupboard on more than one occasion.

With a racing heart she lifted a chair and stood on it and explored the tins and jars with mounting tension. The last tin but one contained a bundle of notes, the size of which she had never seen before, and without scruple Etta reached for it and took it. Payment due for the hard years she had endured!

So far she had made scarcely as much noise as a mouse, but she knew that the worst part yet lay ahead.

She slid the door-bolt back, holding her breath as the rusty bolt emitted a series of strident squeaks. She stood almost petrified, feeling sickly certain that the sounds would be heard and any moment Buck or Cass would appear with a club or a whip or perhaps even a gun.

Slowly the seconds built up into minutes. Then, with a deep gasp, Etta pulled open the outer door and closed it behind her and stood on the night-darkened porch with the sweat of fear moist upon her face and body.

Why was she so afraid, she wondered. She had a gun, and what was to stop her using it if Buck or Cass interfered now? She shook her head. She did not know the answer except that perhaps she could not yet free herself of the sadistic power Weidman had exercised over her for as long as she could recall.

Once clear of the porch, she pulled on her boots and with the gunny sack of food in her left hand walked softly towards the stable.

Three times, recently, Etta had managed to ride the new saddler against the time when she would need every bit of the animal's co-operation; and apart from this, she had fed and groomed it most days.

She swung open the stable door wide enough to allow a shaft of moonlight to shine inside. The roan mare pricked back her ears, and in an instant Etta was at her side stroking the silken muzzle, reassuringly, and talking in low, soothing tones.

Shortly, with the mare wide awake and docile enough, Etta hefted the saddle across its back and cinched it on.

When she had adjusted the bridle and tied the food sack to the saddle, she led the mare outside and quietly closed the stable door.

She cast one last bitter glance at the dark silhouette of the house and began to lead her mount away on to the rough track beside the cornfield.

Not until she had reached the brush-fringed dirt road did the runaway girl vault into the saddle.

With feet firmly in the stirrups and her head flung back to the cool night wind, Etta Storm tasted for the first time the thick and heady wine of complete freedom.

She did not want this wild and wonderful moment to pass and she swore to herself that whatever happened she would never go back to Weidman and his son; not even if they caught up with her and she had to kill.

She orientated herself and rode at a dog-trot. It was not easy, this travelling at night, even with the moon and stars to light her way. But for all the cloistered existence Weidman had forced her to live, Etta was a born frontiers-woman.

She knew exactly where the old Bennet spread lay and she could follow the trails to Brownfield and Mesquite almost with her eyes closed.

Nor did the dismally lonely cry of a coyote concern her overly, or the sudden call of a screech owl in the timber ahead. She had laid awake too many nights hearing these sounds and praying in a pagan-like way that she might exchange them for the sound of Buck Weidman's loathsome voice and the sickening cracking sound of his whip.

She rode on, knowing exactly what she was going to do next and then planning her future moves as carefully as she could.

Yet she was alive to the fact that any small, unforseen thing might well upset her scheme. She was not sure how Oscar Meeks would receive her or whether he might consider it his duty to inform Weidman.

At around two o'clock, Etta swung off the road and put the mare to a series of brush-fringed cut-offs, eventually arriving at a small, sheltered clearing.

She tied the reins to a brush stem and, to make quite sure, hobbled the roan with a short length of rope.

After she had eaten some of the bread and meat, she drank from the canteen which she had been careful to hang on the saddle before setting out. Then, wrapping herself in the single blanket, she lay down and was instantly fast asleep.

As the first pearl grey streaks of dawn began to lighten the eastern sky, Etta arose and quickly gathered brush and sticks for a fire.

She set a coffee pot above the flames and as soon as this was done un-hobbled the roan and led it to a small, almost dried-up creek. Whilst the animal drank, Etta lay full length, dashing the shallow water on to her face and hands until she was clean and refreshed.

She sat hunkered down before the fire, munching her cold breakfast and then washing it down with scalding, bitter coffee. She had not thought to bring sugar with her, but she scarcely noticed how the coffee tasted, so deeply occupied was she with her thoughts.

Less than an hour after awakening, Etta kicked out the fire and covered the remains with alkali dust. She tightened the roan's cinch strap and went into the saddle and rode cross-country towards Mesquite, utterly unaware that yesterday morning the bank here had been held up and two men killed by Frank Sutter and his gang ...

In one way, it was easier to remain inconspicuous in a town as large as Mesquite. There were many more streets than in Brownfield. On the other hand, the population here was thick, and more than once during the early morning Etta had to double back or swing her mount away from the patrolling sheriff and his deputies.

Not being certain where Meeks lived, she had to wait some opportune moment when she might catch him in his office at the Bassett Express Company.

Towards noon, Etta rode her mount to Burr Parker's livery, hoping that the hostler had no reason to remember or recognize the mare. Surely Cass would have paid the horse trader and ridden the mare straight back home. This was one of the many chances she would have to take.

But she need not have worried on that score. She had seen Burr Parker on one or two occasions and the man who came forward now was not Parker.

He said: 'You wanta leave the mare here and have her fed and rubbed down?' He stared hard as he put the question and Etta found herself staring back at this tall, handsome stranger. He was nearly as big as Frank, she realized, but he was dark where Frank was fair and his sun-burned face was lean and angular.

Before she could answer he spoke again and his voice dropped a tone. 'I don't remember ever having seen anyone as pretty as you around town, Miss. My name's Starr—Dave Starr, an' I'm shore glad to meet you!'

He held out a muscular hand and for only a moment Etta hesitated. Then she returned his strong handshake, smiling slightly before she moved back a few paces and removed her dusty stetson and shook her head until the black hair cascaded to her shoulders, shimmering like something alive in the dust-filled sunbeam that slanted across her upper body.

He began lifting bridle and rig from the mare and she watched his every movement as a hawk might watch a rabbit.

'I'm Etta Storm. I—I don't get into Mesquite often. Say, what's happened to Burr Parker?'

He placed saddle and bridle on top of one of the stalls and turned back to her.

'Well, Miss Storm, I guess you wouldn't 've heard about the bank robbery yesterday—?'

Her eyes widened and Dave saw the sudden interest flare into her lovely face. *'Bank Robbery?'*

He nodded. 'Sure. I wasn't around when it happened but it seems a coupla men were killed inside the bank an' Parker had his head split open with a gun-barrel. Anyway, that's what the sheriff an' the doc said.'

'But didn't anyone—?'

'Didn't anyone stop them?'

He smiled tightly. 'They picked a real good time. Got into the bank soon after the teller and cashier had arrived, around eight-forty a.m. or thereabouts—'

'But what about Parker—?'

He shook his head. 'He didn't see who slugged him. A neat job; I'll say that. He didn't even know what had happened until he woke up in the army hospital an' was told.'

'Then—then they got away, whoever it was?'

Dave Starr studied this lovely young girl with the bitter eyes. He wondered where she belonged and what she was doing in Mesquite, apparently alone. She had unfastened the brush jacket against the mounting heat of the day and he saw the butt of a gun protruding from the waistband of her denims.

Her eyes slanted up at him, half angry, half pleased. 'You sure stare a lot, Mr Starr!'

'I'm sorry. I—I was just thinking you seem to be getting a kick out of all this.'

Her eyes widened. 'Well, who wouldn't? 'Tisn't often anything exciting happens. Wonder how much they got away with?'

'Heard tell it was around twenty thousand bucks.' He built a quirly and wiped a match alight and thumbed out the flame with a calloused thumb and forefinger.

He said bluntly: 'Where do you belong, Miss Storm?'

She said almost viciously: 'You don't look like an Easterner an' you don't talk like one. That means you should know better than to ask questions like that!'

Dave took the rebuff with a faint smile. He reckoned he would take most anything from this wild and beautiful creature. She stirred his blood and quickened his interest as no other woman had ever done.

He said mildly: 'I'm not tryin' to pry, Miss Storm, it's just that—well—'

'Mebbe you figger a woman cain't look after herself, Mr Starr! Well, let me tell you, here's one as can.

'If you must know, I rode over to see some folks as live right here in Mesquite!' She swung on her heel and had reached the doors when Dave's soft words stopped her.

'Better do up that brush jacket, Miss Storm.'

She wheeled on him. 'Ain't you ever seen a woman before?'

He shook his head. 'Not like you. But I was thinking about the gun. Sheriff Carter might start askin' you questions—'

'Why should he?'

Dave Starr shrugged and pointed out on to the street where one or two sun-bonneted women with long swirling skirts were shopping. 'Those are the kind of women a Western Peace Officer is used to seein'; not pretty critturs dressed man-fashion an' totin' guns!'

She saw the force of his argument at once and transferred the gun to the right-hand pocket of her open jacket. 'Thanks, Mister. I'll be back for the mare by evening. You be here?'

'Yeah.'

She was half-way out of the livery barn when Dave reached her and touched her lightly on the arm. She swung her face upwards, once more angry at his presumption.

'If there's anything I can do to help you, Etta, let me know,' he said quietly.

She could not understand why he should bother, unless, like Cass and Frank and all men, she supposed, he wanted payment. Yet there was something so utterly resolute and level about his grey eyes that she decided to put it to the test.

She produced several of the bills from her shirt pocket and handed them to him. 'Get me a bottle of whisky, Mr Starr, if you wanta help me.'

'Now see here—'

She rounded on him like a wildcat, her eyes blazing and her lips pulled down at the corners. 'You said you wanted to help me, didn't you? And the first thing I ask you to do, you just stand an' boggle!'

'But—'

'For God's sake spare me the lectures and give me back the money!' She extended her hand and for a long while they stood gazing at each other in silence.

Then Dave pulled his hat down over his eyes and stepped forward. 'Wait here,' he told her quietly, 'I'll be right back.'

CHAPTER SIX

Meeks Does Some Talking

From the moment that Etta had first hit Mesquite, she had had the sense to realize that, dressed as she was in skin-tight denims handed down to her from Cass, she stood out like a sore thumb. Yet she was not sufficiently self-conscious to realize that her good looks and raven black hair were additional qualities to single her out for attention.

But somehow she had managed to keep well clear of Mesquite's townsfolk. All except Dave Starr, that was; and without Dave's help things might have gone differently.

He had brought the whisky back and handed it to her silently, together with the change. He had asked not a single question but had turned to the task of rubbing down the roan mare. He wondered why Etta did not pocket the whisky and walk out there and then, until he remembered his own words about 'pretty critturs dressed man-fashion an' totin' guns.'

Presently he led the roan into a stall, halter-tied it and fed it some oats and hay.

He said: 'Don't you wanta go see your folks?'

She nodded: 'He—he's only a distant relation; my uncle's cousin. Right now he'll be workin'. I bin figurin' it'd be best to see him when he's through for the day.'

'Yeah.' Dave came over to where she squatted on some bales of hay. 'If you don't wanta walk around town, you can stay here 'till you're ready to leave.'

'Supposin' someone comes in here?'

'Likely they will.' He pointed to a dark corner of the stables where clean straw lay on the floor. 'If it makes you feel any better, you can lie down there; mebbe catch a little sleep.'

'Thanks. Aren't you goin' to ask me about the whisky?'

'It's your business, I reckon,' he said drily.

She shook her head. 'You got it for me. You got a right to know. *I* don't touch this stuff. I only bought it for Os—for my uncle's cousin.'

Dave Starr only nodded, but he felt an odd relief deep down inside of him.

Several times during the afternoon, men came in either about their horses or to have a word with the man who was standing in for Burr Parker, but Etta was out of sight and sleeping peacefully beyond the bales of straw.

At around five o'clock, Dave moved across into the hostler's office and brewed some coffee. He poured two cups and carried one to Etta; she awoke the moment he touched her shoulder.

'What time is it?'

'Comin' up to half after five. What time you wanta be movin'?'

'Right now, I reckon.'

She swallowed the hot coffee, looking at him over the rim of the tin cup with a mixture of gratitude and mockery in her dark blue eyes.

She got up, brushing the straw from her clothes while Dave bridled the horse and cinched on the rig.

'You need any directions, Etta?' That was as near as he could get to asking her where she was going.

She lowered her eyes and shook her head. The less folk knew, the less they could talk, and this Dave Starr hombre was no fool, Etta judged.

She mounted and kneed the animal forward to the wide open doors. Then she turned in the saddle and smiled. 'Thanks, Dave,' she said softly, and rode out into the alley towards Main.

This time she had taken care to pile her hair underneath her hat, and despite the warmth she rode with her jacket fastened. She could not pass as a boy, but at least she was not quite so conspicuous especially as there were now quite a few riders and rigs on Main Street.

The Bassett Express Company, she remembered, was located several blocks down, and in a narrow, shadowed alley she sat her mount and waited patiently for Oscar Meeks to appear.

When he did finally emerge from the Express Company's doors, he made straight for a saloon across the way and Etta had another long wait before he came out and trudged towards a lone cottage on the edge of the town.

As he opened the door, something caused him to turn round and see the half-smiling girl astride the roan.

'Oscar! Don't you remember me?'

Meeks was a thin-faced character, prematurely bald and wizened looking. His sallow face was clean shaven save for broad and greying sideburns. He wore a dusty derby on the back of his head, striped trousers and a black frock coat over a fawn vest.

His rather pinched face seemed to fill out as he beamed at this young and beautiful girl without having the slightest idea who she was.

'Last time you saw me, Oscar,' Etta smiled, sliding from the saddle, 'musta bin two years back an' I was bein' close-herded by Buck Weidman.'

His mouth gaped open in astonishment. 'You're not—you're not sayin' you're little Etta—Etta Storm ...?'

She nodded, tied the reins to a fence post and stood waiting for Meeks to open the door.

'Aren't you goin' to invite me in?'

'Why, of course, my dear, of course! Please forgive me, but this is all so unexpected. Come right in and make allowances for the fact that I live alone.'

She surveyed the living room with a critical eye and widely dilated nostrils. The place was dirty, untidy and reeked of tobacco smoke and stale whisky.

'Don't take any notice of the mess,' Meeks apologized, beginning to make some effort to clear up the room. 'Like I said, you must make allowances—'

'Sure.' Already Etta felt that she had this miserable creature in the palm of her hand and when she handed him the bottle of whisky she sensed that her task should not be too difficult.

'I sure am glad you're not one of

109

these mealy-mouthed females, Etta, who begrudge a man a drink now and again. Why, you couldn't 've brought me anything better. Sit down now, while I fix us somethin' to eat. You will stay and have supper?'

'Why not?' Etta smiled and took off her coat. 'Mebbe I can give you a hand?'

The kitchen was a small ante-room leading from the main living room, and while Meeks lit the stove and began preparations, Etta opened the bottle of whisky.

'Here, have a drink now. It'll give you an appetite for supper.'

Meeks grinned wolfishly. 'You'll find a coupla glasses in the cupboard yonder. This is something of a celebration, so I'll expect you to join me!'

Whatever else, Etta knew that she would have to keep her wits about her. Oscar Meeks seemed harmless enough right now, but looks could be deceptive, as well she knew from both Weidman and Cass.

She poured a stiff dose for Meeks and, under cover of rinsing the glasses under the pump in the sink, watered her own until it was well nigh impotent.

By the time the meal was ready, Oscar Meeks' eyes were already blood-shot and his step uncertain ...

'You've sure grown into a fine gal, Etta. Tell me! How's Buck bin treatin' you of late and, for that matter, how come you visited me all on your lonesome?' He reached out and put an arm around her waist, but with an adroit movement Etta twisted free.

'Later, Oscar. First, let's talk a while. I wanta hear all about your excitin' job; all the valuable shipments you send off every week. It—it all seems so wonderful to me!'

She had touched the right chord. Even Oscar's drinking was forgotten for a while as he regaled this innocent girl with tales of big gold shipments and other valuables which the Bassett Express Company had successfully delivered on schedule.

'But aren't the coaches ever waylaid by road-agents or—or outlaws?' Etta asked, wide-eyed.

Meeks grinned. 'Once—twice, things like that has happened, but we got good drivers and shot-gun guards who know the routes like their own back yards—'

'But what about these hold-ups? Haven't you *ever* lost anything?'

'Oh, sure. I remember once when a stage was held up by a band of masked men and the driver and guard shot dead—'

She leaned towards him, her face alight with excitement. 'What happened, Oscar?'

He was pretty drunk now and the whisky in the bottle was low. Yet, except for his slow speech and his reddened eyes, he showed little signs of his heavy drinking.

He reached forward and grasped her arms, placing his moist mouth on hers, and inwardly Etta fought against the nausea of his embrace.

She had known all along that she would have to give this man some latitude if she were to obtain any vital information. This, she thought with a dismal bitterness, was her only weapon, just as it had been with Cass ...

Laughingly, Etta pushed Meeks away

and placed a finger on her mouth as though to guard those inviting lips at least temporarily.

As for Meeks, he was aware but vaguely of the girl's strength and leaned back almost sulkily until, with honeyed words, she prodded him back to talking.

'You haven't told me what happened, Oscar, dear. About that stage hold-up, I mean!'

'Oh, that. Yeah, I'd almost forgotten what we were talking about; you're so damned pretty and—'

'Later, Oscar. You know a woman's always interested in a man as important as you; a man who helps plan the stage schedules—'

He grinned widely. 'My job ain't all that important, Etta. All I haveta do is take in the merchandize, arrange for tickets and receipts and such like an' warn the drivers and guards beforehand when they're going to haul something big.'

'Like a gold shipment, you mean?'

He nodded and drained his glass, smacking his lips and staring into space while he collected his thoughts.

'As a matter of fact, Etta, we're shipping a payroll this Saturday—'

'To where?'

'Oh.' He loosened the collar of his shirt and wiped his perspiring face. Then he turned and stared at her glassily. 'What's it matter—?'

'Where's it going from, Oscar? And where's it going to? You don't mind tellin' me, do you? Why, I'm a relative!'

It was becoming increasingly difficult for Meeks to focus on anything except this girl's lovely face and the tanned neck and shoulders that showed beneath her open-necked shirt.

'Stage is leavin' Mesquite at eight on Saturday an' is haulin' ten thousand dollars to Cottonwood Junction. That what you wanted to know? Now, how about another kiss, Etta—?'

She reached for the bottle and handed it to him, smiling enigmatically.

'Finish it up, Oscar. We can allus get some more!'

The idea seemed to please him and he

put the neck to his mouth and took down the fiery spirit at a single gulp. Etta Storm held her breath.

Slowly Meeks' head lolled back on the horsehair sofa and in a few minutes he was snoring gently.

Etta stood looking down at the man on the sofa as he breathed stertorously through his drunken sleep.

She felt no pity or compassion. She did not care what happened to men like Buck Weidman and Oscar Meeks. All she felt at the moment was a surge of elation, of triumph, that so far her plan had worked more quickly than she had dared to hope.

One thought bothered the girl as she picked up her coat and put it on. *Would Meeks remember what he had told her, when he awoke; and if so, would he try and alter the stage coach schedule for Saturday?*

Somehow, looking at him now, Etta doubted whether Meeks was the kind of man to admit his own failures. For surely if he *did* try to alter the departure time, questions would be asked by the driver and shot-gun guard. In that case, Meeks would have to lie his way out by saying he had received an anonymous tip-off that the stage was going to be held up.

What then? Likely as not, the driver and guard would press for more details; they might even laugh at Meeks and shrug the whole thing off. Men who had tooled stages over deserts, across mountains and badlands, facing attacks by Indians or outlaws, did not scare easily at the mention of some vague tip-off.

Thus Etta reasoned as she tidied up the place, carefully washing her own glass and dishes and leaving Meeks' greasy plate untouched and the empty glass and bottle on the floor.

Satisfied at length that she had left no sign of her own presence there, Etta quietly opened and shut the rear door and walked around the side of the house and waited for a long moment in the shadows of late evening.

A man's footsteps sounded loud and clear on the hard-packed path across the way and Etta considered whether he would see the tied mare in the now fast descending darkness and wonder at it.

But whoever was across the street appeared to be in a hurry to reach the well-lit and noisy section of Main. The footfalls faded away and Etta came out from the cast shadows and untied the mare and went into the saddle without a second's delay.

She threaded her way through a labyrinth of mean side streets and overgrown lots and eventually hit Main and thus orientated herself from there.

A half-hour later she was well clear of Mesquite and its drab outskirts and cutting through brush and along boulder-fringed trails towards the distant Bennet spread ...

The stars were bright and the moon, save for a few scudding clouds, was her clear and infallible compass. She did not spare herself or the mare, determined to reach Sutter's place well before midnight. As she rode, she ate some of the remaining food in her sack, wondering now whether

Frank would accept her; whether Weidman would search for her. Lastly, she thought of the dark, good-looking Dave Starr who had temporarily taken over Burr Parker's job. Was he a citizen of Mesquite, she wondered, or just a wandering grubline rider who had jumped at the chance of earning a few easy dollars?

At length, Etta hit a shallow creek which she crossed and, knowing this section, she put the roan to the grassy ridge ahead.

In the moonlight she could make out the dark shape of the Bennet home buildings, and from the house several lights showed brightly yellow against the indigo blue of the night.

She came into the yard and hauled up at the porch; dismounted and tied her mount's reins to the rail.

She had climbed the porch steps when a figure loomed up out of the shadows, grasping her arm in a grip that made her wince.

Etta held herself rigid and forced back the cry of pain which sprang to her lips. She said through clenched teeth: 'Take me to Frank Sutter an' be darn quick, Mister!'

Jesse Lindquist was surprised to learn that he had caught a girl. Yet he was not slow to absorb the fierce urgency in her words and the way she spat them out.

'Take it easy, Sister,' he snarled, and pushed her unhurriedly into the house.

Frank, Jim and Lonny were seated at the table and another man whom she did not know leaned back in a chair, reading.

She felt their gazes lift and beat against her as she stood in the strong lamplight, the bearded man still holding her arm.

'You got a visitor, Frank,' Lindquist drawled. 'She comes ridin' in demanding to see Frank Sutter!'

'Hallo, Etta.' Frank nodded at Lindquist and the latter released Etta's arm. She rubbed the bruised flesh gently. 'I didn't come here to be man-handled by your men, Frank. I—'

'Why did you come, Etta?'

She laid her gaze on each and every one in turn and returned stare for stare with a boldness that impressed these hard-case men.

Frank Sutter could see that something of a transformation had taken place within Etta Storm. Here was no helpless girl afraid of her uncle's wrath. Instead, she stood amongst these gun-men now, alone and unafraid as though she were one of them.

'It's all right, Etta, you can talk freely. You've seen Lonny an' Jim here. The man behind you is Jesse Lindquist an' that's Cal Selwyn over there.'

She said slowly: 'How'd you like to earn yourselves ten thousand dollars for an hour or two's work, Frank?'

She stood very straight and tall before them, her head lifted high and the semblance of a smile upon her lips. There was no sound inside the room for a moment until Frank's rumbling laugh broke the crawling silence.

'You allus was determined you'd help us, Etty, wasn't you?' he said smiling. 'I got an idea you might be serious about this.'

He turned his blue gaze on to Lindquist and then Selwyn who had laid his newspaper aside. 'This is Etta Storm, boys, niece of that ole buzzard Buck Weidman I told you about. An' don't be fooled jest 'cause Etta's scarce outa school. She can use that Colt dam' near as well as you, Lonny.'

Selwyn said: 'How do we know this ain't some kind've trick, Frank?'

'Because,' Etta replied through her teeth. 'I ain't givin' Frank any more information 'till he's promised me two things and one of those things is that I ride with you an' take the same risks as you-all do!'

Lonny said softly: 'On the face of it, that sounds fair enough, but it could still be a trick.'

Etta strode across the room and placed her hands on the table, staring hard at Lonny.

'Look, Mister—'

'All right!' It was Frank's cool but firm voice that interrupted. 'I know Etta and,' he added, grinning, 'I can vouch for the fact she's no lawman!'

The room rocked with their laughter and Etta stood there, face madder-tinged, waiting patiently for her turn.

'So,' Frank went on presently, 'you wanta ride with us, Etty! Mebbe that could be arranged. What was the other thing?'

'I pulled up stakes last night, Frank. I ain't ever goin' back to Buck Weidman's place. If he or Cass should come here lookin' for me, I want you to send 'em hot-footin' it back!'

'If them dam' nesters figger they can ask us *any* questions,' Frank murmured, 'they'll likely finish up eatin' lead! All right, Etty. What's the play?'

'Don't you reckon we oughta have all the boys in on this, Frank?' Jim Sutter asked.

Frank stood up, towering above everyone in the room. He leaned his broad shoulders against the wall and hooked his thumbs into his belt.

'First off, let's hear what the girl's got to say. If it's as good as it sounds, we can call Doc and the others in later.'

CHAPTER SEVEN

Stage Hold-up

Dave Starr's thoughts and feelings were mixed up considerably as he watched Etta Storm ride from the livery. At the back of his mind were the first faint stirrings of doubt, but first and foremost, he told himself, he was concerned with this beautiful young girl's safety.

Yet several small things she had said, as well as her behaviour, were a little suspect, Dave thought, as he quickly threw bridle and rig on to his steel-dust and rode out on to the street.

Why had she not come out with the name of her uncle's cousin, for instance? It would have been the most natural thing in the world to do this. And why did a young girl have to take a bottle of rye when she visited the man? Was it to pacify him? If so, what kind of a side-winder was he and why did Etta have to go and see him anyway?

Dave was new enough to Mesquite not to know many folks, but he did know the West and generally it was no place for a lovely young girl to be sashaying around on her lonesome.

Besides which, she had touched some hidden spring inside Dave Starr; something he had not even known existed ...

Trailing Etta was as easy to Dave Starr as falling off a log. The fact that she was keeping to side-streets and alleys did not surprise him in view of their earlier conversation ...

By the time she finally reined in, in a narrow, shadowy alley, Dave was beginning to feel intrigued by the whole business. Obviously the girl was waiting for someone, but surely this furtiveness was carrying things too far. Besides which it did not seem in keeping with the half-wild defiance she had displayed in the livery.

He could see a small part of Main Street at the end of the alley where Etta waited as still and patient as an Indian. He fell to figuring what particular buildings were in the vicinity and gave it up when he had mentally counted three saloons, a dozen stores and one dance hall.

Of a sudden he saw the girl swing away from the alley and put her mount to the street at a slow walk. Almost immediately she plunged into a network of narrower side-streets. At this point, Dave dismounted and ground-tied the steel-dust and went along on foot until Etta stopped outside a run-down house. She was talking to the man whom, Dave now realized, she had been following. He did not know the fellow's name but he remembered having seen him in the offices of the Bassett Express Company.

Starr dare not get too close, but after a short while Etta went inside with the man, leaving her horse tied outside.

Was this her uncle's cousin, the whisky wallower? Dave wondered, and if so, why the secrecy?

He determined to play out this hand, however long it took and whatever turned up. The livery would have to look after itself ...

With the approach of dusk, Dave was able to get a little nearer to the house, keeping himself well covered by the darkening shadows between two shacks almost opposite.

He heard a door open and close quietly and he drew back as a man tromped past him within a few feet. Shortly afterwards, Dave saw the girl appear from the side of the house, glance around and mount up quickly. In a moment she was being swallowed up in the gathering darkness.

All Dave's instincts exhorted him to continue following the girl. But his training told him that he might uncover more of the mystery if he searched the house.

He quickly found the back door through which, he judged, Etta must have emerged. Why had she not used the front door?

He struck a match and groped around until he had found and lit a lamp. He was in a dirty, smelly kitchen, and odours of a recently cooked meal still hung on the air.

He went through into the living room and lit another lamp, and when he turned he saw a man lying full length on the sofa and breathing heavily.

Dave noticed the empty bottle and picked it up, examining it carefully. It looked like the same bottle he had bought for Etta earlier on.

He looked around further and was more and more puzzled by what he found. A meal had been cooked, but there was evidence that only one person had eaten; presumably the man who was now in a drunken sleep. Surely Etta would have eaten *something*, Dave thought, or was she trying hard to cover her tracks?

He rummaged around in a bureau and found several letters and papers which indicated that the man in the living room was Oscar Meeks, employee of the Bassett Express Company.

Dave pushed back his hat and rolled and fired a quirly, not caring much whether Meeks should wake up and demand an explanation.

He sat there for quite a time, smoking

and thinking and wondering where the hell all this was getting him and whether it was really part of his job to pry into the secret lives of folk like Meeks and Etta Storm.

Right now, Dave reflected, he would give a month's pay to know where Etta had gone and what her game was, if any.

Trouble was, Dave Starr had nothing to go on as far as Etta was concerned; nothing concrete at least. All that could be said was that her behaviour was secretive and odd. But there could be many innocent explanations to such actions and because a person behaved oddly they were by no means necessarily criminal.

Even the fact that the girl had presumably left Meeks in a drunken sleep meant little enough. Likely the man had gotten drunk and, disgusted at his condition, Etta had quietly ridden away.

Dave got up and ground out his cigarette. He thought of waking Meeks up and questioning him, but he had no legal right to do this and decided that it would serve little purpose anyway.

After a while, Dave Starr left the house,

re-traced his steps to where he had left the steel-dust and made his slow, thoughtful way back to the livery.

There was a sourness in his belly when he thought of the miles he had covered tailing the Sutter gang. This feeling was in no way mitigated by his belief that Frank and his brothers were the ones who had robbed the bank. Yet there was not one shred of evidence which Dave could produce to substantiate any accusations ...

It was early morning when Meeks finally awoke, with a splitting headache and a mouth as dry as the desert.

He got up stiffly, shivered and yawned and made for the kitchen, pumping water on to his face and hands until the shock of it had restored him to some semblance of normal cohesion.

He pulled back the curtains and turned down the lamps which had been left burning and only then did memory of the previous evening flood through Meeks' now awakened being.

So Etta had walked out on him! He began to remember things now, such as the whisky, for instance, and he bent down and picked up the empty bottle and opened the rear door and flung it on the trash heap outside.

He shaved and combed his sparse hair, all the while thinking about the fiasco last night and wondering more and more about Etta Storm.

At a little before seven-thirty, Oscar Meeks left the house and made his way towards Main Street and the Company's office. Today the stage would be leaving at eight o'clock or thereabouts and he had to be there to deal with freight and passengers ...

Towards afternoon, Meeks found that he was concentrating less and less on his work and more and more on the events of last night. There was a vague idea floating around at the back of his mind and eventually something clicked in his brain and he sat there in a cold sweat, shivering at the thought which had finally clarified itself.

Etta had asked him questions about the stage schedule *and suddenly he had recalled what he had told her about the gold shipment!*

Oh, God! Surely she could not be mixed up with any road-agents! Not Etta Storm, of all people! Yet why had she pressed him for details of Saturday's haul? What a fool he had been to tell her! If the news ever reached the ears of Art Black, the section manager, it might well cost Meeks his job. Such information was highly confidential.

Oscar got up from his desk, shaking and sweating. He reached inside the back of a cupboard and withdrew a half-pint bottle of rye and took a long swig. He shuddered as the neat spirit coursed through him and then, suddenly, he felt much better.

What kind of thinking was this? He was behaving like an idiot. Etta was Buck's niece, a nester girl who helped work Weidman's land and fetched and carried for him. That much Oscar Meeks knew without doubt.

Why, it was just as crazy to imagine that Sheriff Carter or his two deputies or

Mayor Mayard were planning some foul deed! Obviously, Etta was interested in what went on in the outside world. She had little enough contact with it, Oscar imagined, with Cousin Buck and Cass always keeping a tight rein on the kid!

Meeks felt much better now as he returned to his desk. He could not imagine why such a crazy and impossible notion had ever come to him in the first place ...

Yet during the next two days, the nagging thought came back again and again. He found it difficult to answer straightforward questions or even make out the tickets correctly for Saturday's stage run to Cottonwood Junction.

Maybe he should drop Art Black a hint; cook up some plausible story which would put the Company on their guard and give them a chance to protect themselves—just in case!

Not that Oscar Meeks cared two hoots about the Express Company or the payrolls they shipped, but he did care about his job and his own skin ...

132

Early Saturday morning, a small band of riders trotted out from the Lazy S spread, heading towards a certain spot on the Mesquite—Cottonwood Junction stage road.

The group comprised the three Sutter boys, Etta, Doc Dufresne, Brad Keiler, Jack Munroe and Clint Lawler; the rest of Sutter's gang were staying put at the ranch.

Etta rode a brown gelding; the roan mare might be too easily identifiable.

She spurred her mount alongside Frank as Dufresne rode on to scout the way ahead.

'Don't forget what I said about Meeks, Frank,' the girl warned. 'If he *did* remember what he told me, then mebbe this thing won't be such a cinch. Mebbe they'll run a decoy coach or somethin'!'

Frank smiled. 'You got brains, Etta, as well as beauty. I got to admit that. But don't worry, everythin'll be taken care of, whether the Bassett Express Company's plannin' a surprise or not.'

She nodded, content now to leave things in the capable hands of Frank and these tough riders of his. But she wished she knew more about Meeks and the kind of man he was; whether he would remember and warn his employers even at the risk of involving himself or perhaps losing his job.

The place Frank had selected on the stage road was a perfect spot for an ambush. For a short distance on either side of this stretch, brush and boulder-rock walled the road. Moreover at this point the trail ascended a fairly steep gradient so that a stage coach or even a rider would be forced to go at a slow gait.

Once Dufresne had returned with the news that the way ahead was clear, the outlaws gathered round Frank for their final instructions. Lonny was the only one to protest.

'I still don't like the idea of pullin' this stunt so soon after the bank at Mesquite,' he said, his dark glance switching from Frank to Etta. 'Mebbe—'

'Mebbe you'd best shut up, Lonny,'

Frank said quietly, 'an' listen to what we's gonna do.'

'That's the talk, Frank,' Abe Dufresne chuckled. 'Are we so goddam rich we can afford to pass up ten thousand bucks?'

Lonny scowled but said nothing.

Frank waited a moment, then pointed to some flat rocks across to the other side of the trail.

'I want you, Doc, an' Clint to belly down atop them rocks an' keep your hosses under cover. You, Jim, will be in the brush directly under Doc an' Clint. That way the coach'll be covered from two different levels on that side.'

He turned to Lonny. 'You an' Munroe will do likewise, Lonny, on this side of the road, over to them rocks yonder, see? While Brad bellies down in the brush below you.'

Lonny grinned, his former discontent swept aside by his brother's carefully worked out details. 'Reckon it can hardly miss, Frank, even if them bastards *do* know what to expect.'

Frank grinned coolly. 'They may've bin

tipped off or not; either way I don't care, because you'll take the nearest lead horse, soon as they hit the gradient an' slow down; an' you, Doc, will take the other lead horse. That'll stop the coach. At the same time you're doin' that, me an' Etta will take the driver an' guard apart.'

'Where do we come in?' Keiler asked. 'Me an' Munroe, I mean?'

'We ain't takin' chances on this trip,' Frank said, 'so while we's all stoppin' the coach an' knockin' off the driver and guard, you an' Munroe'll be pourin' lead in through the windows!'

Etta said in a choked kind of voice: 'You mean you ain't goin' to give anyone a chance to throw up his hands?'

Jim said coldly: 'Mebbe you'd like to try holdin' up the coach on your loncsome, Etta, an' see whether they'll hesitate to fill your belly up with hot lead!'

Frank said: 'You wanted in on this, Etty? You ain't changed your mind?'

She swallowed hard and shook her head. 'I said I'd take orders from you, Frank, an' I will, whatever they are—'

'Then the first thing you can do is pile that hair of yours underneath your hat and button up that jacket. We don't want any slip-ups, even though I don't figure there'll be anyone left to identify us!'

Frank glanced at the climbing sun as Dufresne took a watch from his pocket. 'Stage should've left Mesquite nigh on half an hour ago. That right, Doc? Okay then: you boys get to your places an' see your hosses are secure.'

Etta and Frank sat their mounts in a stand of young cottonwoods while the men rode to their positions.

Frank wiped the sweat from his face and grinned down at Etta.

'Reckon you could almost pass for a boy, with your hair dragged tight back like that. Almost!'

Etta nodded absently, her mind on more important things. She had schemed hard for this day and had run risks. She had achieved her first goal, namely to be riding with Frank on a hold-up; and the information for which had been supplied by herself.

Now, despite Frank's careful, ruthless planning, she began to feel uncertain. She tried to keep the fear of failure from showing in her eyes.

Sutter built and fired a quirly and passed the cigarette to Etta. Almost mechanically she took two or three quick puffs and then handed it back.

He was stubbing the butt out on his saddle-horn when his head lifted sharply.

'Stage is comin', Etty. Better pull up that neck-piece.'

She did as she was bidden, realizing that her whole body was damp with sweat and that her limbs were shaking.

Frank raised his arm, signalling to Doc across the road. Dufresne acknowledged the signal and for the next fifteen minutes or so Etta went through one of the worst times in her whole life. She wondered how this could possibly be any better than enduring Weidman's whip, and then the coach was breasting the distant ridge and all such thoughts left Etta as she drew and cocked her pistol and prepared for action.

The stage coach came careering along the road until it was forced to a slower pace by the gradient. All the bushwhackers were able to see the driver and guard quite clearly, perched high on the box like sitting ducks. At one moment the only sounds breaking the peaceful quiet of the morning were those of crunching wheels and pounding hooves and the sailing voice of the stage driver as he urged the team to their uphill climb.

Then, with shocking abruptness, these sounds were overridden by the vicious crack of rifles.

Etta saw the far lead horse go down, then the nearer one. The remainder of the team reared up in panic, almost overturning the coach.

More bullets screamed from the brush and the driver, clutching at his breast, keeled over from the box and crashed in the billowing dust of the road.

Already the shot-gun guard had loosed off one barrel, but he had no clear target on which to sight and before he could discharge the second barrel into the brush he, too, toppled over, falling half across the box and, by some remote chance, remaining in a grotesquely reclining position.

Frank was already spurring from the sheltering brush and Etta was not slow to follow, despite the fact that a veritable fusillade of shots was coming at them from inside the coach.

But whoever it was, crouched down there on the floor of the vehicle, they had little enough chance, cornered as they were in a cross-fire and with two more guns coming at them from ahead.

Perhaps it was Frank Sutter's natural incapacity for experiencing any kind of fear; or perhaps he figured that the battle was already over and finished with. At all events, he spurred recklessly close to the coach door, gun held aloft.

For a brief moment a man's head and shoulders showed at the open windows of the coach and a long-barrelled Colt's gun winked in the sunlight.

Pale orange blossomed from the muzzle and lead tore into the big, masked figure of Frank, knocking him from the saddle.

Lonny and Jim and one other man were running forward now, but in a flash Etta levelled her own pistol and fired.

Through the back-drift of powder-smoke she saw the man in the coach jerk convulsively and then disappear from view. Instinctively she knew he was not playing 'possum'; she had killed her first man and the thought was at once both frightening and exhilarating.

Doc, Lonny, Jim and the rest were all crowding forward and for some indefinable reason or instinct they all looked to Etta for a lead.

Was it because she was literally above them, being the only one mounted; or because it was she who had ridden at Frank's stirrup into that short, sharp fusillade of lead?

Etta said: 'Doc! Frank's hurt! Can you get him back and tend his wound?'

For a moment Dufresne hesitated before hurrying across to where Frank Sutter had fallen. Quickly he staunched the flow of blood and, with Lonny's help, got the wounded outlaw leader back into the saddle.

Again, Etta took the initiative and again, curiously enough, she was not questioned.

'Jim! Get the strong box down from up there!'

Clint Lawler came forward to help, while Munroe and Keiler inspected the inside of the coach, guns in hand.

It was Etta's gun that blew the lock off the strong box and, hurriedly, Lonny and the others transferred gold pokes and bundles of notes to their saddlebags. By now, Dufresne was out of sight, helping the half-conscious Frank back to the ranch ...

CHAPTER EIGHT

Chance of Death

From nearly a mile back, where the road curved at the ridge, Dave Starr sat his horse, watching the scene down the trail, powerless to intervene.

He reached into his saddlebag for a field glass, placing it to his eye and careful to keep the lens away from the sun's oblique rays.

He was fairly sure that the big man who had been hit and then helped to ride off was Frank Sutter. This raid had all the earmarks of a Sutter job, Starr thought bitterly. Shooting the stage riders down in cold blood; that was typical.

And then Dave held his breath as he focused on the rider who seemed to be running things in the absence of Frank. For, despite the fact that the face was masked, there was no mistaking that slim figure clad in denims, brush jacket and stetson!

Dave knew that he could not be mistaken. Had he not had ample opportunity to study Etta Storm at close quarters during that afternoon she had spent in the livery?

Starr was pretty tough. A man who went after killers had to be. But the knowledge that the lovely black-haired girl was presumably a member of Sutter's gang momentarily held Dave quite still.

Only his eyes moved as he saw the small cavalcade of outlaws swing off the road and plunge out of sight into the brush. While he waited out the minutes, Dave built and lit a quirly and later stubbed it out and knew that it was time to move.

He rode at an easy lope, careful not to throw up a banner of dust, yet he feared that time no longer mattered to the men of the Bassett Express Company; and as soon as he rode up he knew he had been right. Trust Sutter and his men to make sure there were no witnesses left to testify!

Dave dismounted and one quick look at the driver showed him that the man was dead. He glanced up at the box, seeing the shot-gun guard and knowing from the grotesque position of his body and the utter stillness of the man that he, too, was beyond human aid.

Dave's eyes went past the guard, his gaze reaching up into the sky and seeing the wheeling black specks growing larger as they slowly descended in spiral fashion.

He did not relish this chore; it was a

grisly business but it had to be done. Now, as though scenting the buzzards, the four horses were lunging, their eyes bloodshot, white foam caked upon their muzzles.

Dave rammed the brake down hard before opening the stage coach door. He stepped back quickly as a man fell out headlong and lay stark and still in the dust. He was still clutching a Colt's gun in his right hand.

A fourth man law sprawled on the floor of the coach, a Spencer carbeen near his hand. Part of his face had been shot away, and even the tough Dave Starr winced and turned to his horse and pulled a half-pint bottle from his saddle pocket.

He took a long swig and felt much, much better and set to work to clear things up.

He laid the two special guards on one seat and carried the bodies of the driver and the shot-gun guard separately, laying them on the opposite seat. That done, he cut the ribbons and traces of the dead lead horses and climbed on to the box and managed to wheel the team, making a U turn on the road.

Finally, Dave tied his own mount to the rear of the coach and then began the task of driving his grim freight back to Mesquite and the Bassett Express Company.

Somewhere around the middle of the forenoon, Dave Starr tooled the four-horse stage down Main Street and hauled up outside the Express Office ...

Dave figured there would be an inquest over the whole business. Not only on account of the dead men who had been employed by the Express Company—though that was serious enough—but also on account of what had gone wrong and why.

Why, for instance, had this Dave Starr been Johnny-on-the-spot if he were not in cahoots with the robbers?

Not that anyone had come out with a direct accusation, but Art Black had made one or two veiled remarks even at this early stage in the proceedings.

Sheriff Jack Carter turned his swivel chair so that he was facing Art Black. 'How come the stage wasn't carrying passengers,

Art; leastways, only a couple of special messengers? It means, doesn't it, that you was tipped off about this raid?'

Black took a stogie from his pocket, bit at the end and lit it with a sulphur match, shaking his head.

'Hardly what you'd call a tip-off, Sheriff. If it had bin, I'd 've arranged for more men—'

Jake Sepple asked: 'How much did you know, Art?'

'Hell-an'-be-merry! It was only somethin' Oscar Meeks said. Even then I guess I didn't take the thing real serious. I only wish I had. Coles an' Forrest were dam' good men an' ol' man Bassett ain't goin' to like this one little bit!'

'What did Meeks tell you?' Carter demanded irritably. 'For God's sake, Art, cain't you get to the point?'

'It was Thursday evening when I saw Meeks,' Black said thoughtfully. 'He was kinda nervous and on edge and I asked him if anythin' was the matter.' Art took a puff at his stogie and continued.

He said: 'Meeks gave me some yarn

about finding a warning note at his house; said it must've bin shoved under the door when he was asleep.'

'When did Oscar Meeks find this note?' Dave Starr enquired mildly.

Black lifted his shoulders and Carter snapped: 'More important, what did the note say?'

'Oscar told me it was a warnin' that today's stage would be held up an' the payroll snatched. When I asked him for the note, Meeks said he had taken it as some kind of prank, that he'd destroyed the paper—'

'Then why—'

'Apparently it began preying on his mind,' Art Black replied. 'I guess many folk have second thoughts about things and the nearer it got to Saturday, the more worried Meeks became. So he upped an' told me!'

'And you put a coupla extra guards in the coach, in place of the passengers?' Jack Carter asked.

'Yeah. I was inclined to figger things the same way as Meeks; that some kid or other had written the note for sheer devilment.'

'But you took precautions,' Jack Sepple interposed.

'Sure I did. You-all know that now. But at the time, I felt someone was out to make a fool of me or the Company. I figgered that if Bassett found out I'd cancelled bookings and refunded money all for some fool prank, there'd be the deuce to pay.'

Carter nodded, tugging at his longhorn moustache. 'Yeah. I can see that, Art. In any case there wasn't much time for you to do anything.'

'No, there wasn't. I was able to find Coles an' Forrest on Friday and by early Saturday both they and the regular driver and guard was warned to be on the look-out. Short of cancelling the run, I couldn't do no more.'

Carter turned and laid his cold gaze on Dave Starr. 'Tell us your story, Mr Starr, and how you came to be—'

'I told you once already, Sheriff,' Dave said patiently.

'Then tell us again. Mebbe there was

something you left out; some little thing you forgot about!'

The time involved during all this talk in the Sheriff's office, apart from the hour or so driving the stage back to Mesquite, had given Dave opportunity enough to prepare his story with consummate care.

He shoved the stetson well back on his head, revealing more clearly his darkly tanned face.

'Like I said, Sheriff. It was just that I'd heard of a man in Brownfield who was lookin' for riders. Well, as I told you the first day I hit Mesquite, I'm a cowpuncher—'

'Sure,' the sheriff said testily. 'I ain't interested in all that, an' how you bin lookin' after the livery. What I wanta know is how come you saw the hold-up an'—'

'Just a blind chance, is all,' Starr smiled. 'I figured eight o'clock as good a time as any to set out, an' as I was not too sure of the trails I took the stage road, intending to branch off someplace an' head for Brownfield.'

'All right,' Carter growled. 'So you was

there by accident. What did you see?'

'First off, some long while after the stage had passed me—I was ridin' slow an' easy, you understand—I heard shots.

'I spurred my horse forward, but not too fast as by the amount of gun-fire it sounded like there was a small army up ahead.'

'What then?'

'I was approaching a ridge an' I figgered the best thing to do was quit the trail an' take to the brush. Sure as hell, soon as I could see down the road, I made out mebbe a dozen or so masked figures. They sure didn't waste any time shootin' the lock off that strong-box an' then high-tailin' it!'

'Which way?'

Dave shrugged broad shoulders. 'Once they was beyond the brush and the rocks, I couldn't see 'em. They might've headed in any direction.

'I waited a spell, just to make sure they wasn't around, then I rode up to see if there was anything I could do.'

'None of the Express men were still alive

then?' Art Black asked.

Starr shook his head. 'Whoever robbed that stage made sure there was no witnesses—'

'But what about you, Starr?' The sheriff demanded. 'Couldn't you identify any o' them killers?'

The sun-burned stranger thought about this for a while. Then he said: 'Well, Sheriff, even usin' my field glass, I couldn't see much. Like I said, they was all masked an' all rode dark horses without any obvious markings, far as I could see.'

'My guess is that it's the same gang as robbed the bank only last Monday mornin',' Carter said. 'Well, Starr,' he continued, 'I reckon we're all obliged to you for doin' what you could—'

Dave stood up. 'It was little enough. I wish I could've told you more. Right now I wanta get into Brownfield, Sheriff. You want me any more?'

Carter shook his head. 'I guess we haven't got anything on you, Starr. Just so long as you get back here by tomorrow noon. The coroner might need your evidence at the inquest.'

Dave nodded. 'I'll be back,' he said, and stepped from the sheriff's office on to the boardwalk and built a quirly.

He stood for a while, wondering why the sheriff had not thought of the Sutter boys; for Carter ought to know that they were raising cattle a dozen miles away. Maybe he *did* know, Dave thought, and was purposely keeping tight-mouthed.

Dave ground the butt of his quirly under his boot, climbed into the saddle and headed from town, careful to see that he was not being followed ...

Frank Sutter lay stretched out on two tables in a back room of the ranch house.

Lonny and Jim were dark, watching figures beyond the lamplight under which Doc and Etta worked.

Presently Doc Dufresne stepped back with a deep sigh. 'You did well, Etta. Ain't many women who'd stand up to a job like that as cool as you did.'

'How is he, Doc? Will he be all right?'

153

Etta placed the lamp she had been holding on a nearby cabinet and Lonny and Jim came forward, their glances sober and questioning on Abe Dufresne's face.

The medico nodded. 'Frank's as tough as an ox. He—' But Sutter's eyes were open now and he stared dully up at the faces which seemed to be hovering over him.

'Where am I?' he croaked. 'What happened?'

'It's all right, Frank,' Abe said. 'I just got a slug outa you with Etta's help. You'll be right as rain in a few weeks—'

'A few weeks hell! I ain't stayin' outa circulation for that length of time!'

Etta said: 'Take it easy, Frank. Doc knows what's best for you.' She caught hold of the whisky bottle standing near the lamp and held it to Frank Sutter's lips. 'Take another swig; it'll make you feel a sight better.'

Sutter took a long pull, handed the bottle back and, despite Doc's protests, painfully struggled to a sitting position.

'Lonny! Jim! You both all right?'

'Sure.' Lonny grinned. 'You was the unlucky one. No one else got a scratch—'

'You wouldn't 've bin so lucky if it hadn't bin for Etta here,' Jim said. 'Doc'll vouch for that!'

Frank passed a hand over his sweating brow. 'I seem to remember now. Etty an' me was ridin' up to the coach when a gun poked out an' a slug hit me like a bolt of lightnin'!'

Dufresne nodded. 'It's like Jim said. Etta sure saved your hide. I ain't ever seen a woman as cool as she was, facin' those slugs—'

'I guess I owe you my thanks, Etty,' Frank said slowly, his eyes on the black-haired girl. 'I told Lonny you could use that .36 of yours an' by God you can!'

'Listen, boys. Mebbe I'll haveta take things easy for a bit, if that's what the Doc says. Meanwhile, Lonny, you're the boss if it comes to any action an' I want you to keep Etta by your side—'

'Sure, Frank. But you ain't plannin' anythin' more for a while, are you?'

'Who knows! If I don't think up

somethin' I'll go crazy, jest sittin' around here waitin' for this wound to heal. How about the money?'

Doc said: 'We got that all right. Ten thousand bucks, just like Etta said. But we spent a tidy sum on cattle and hosses recently.'

Sutter nodded. 'All the more reason why we gotta think up somethin' real good for the next raid—'

A knock sounded at the door and Munroe came in, looking first at Etta and then at Sutter still seated on the tables.

'Glad to see you sittin' up, Frank. Say, there's a pilgrim name o' Weidman outside. He's askin' to see you—'

'Leave this to me, Frank,' Lonny said, hitching up his gun belt and moving forward.

'I reckon I'd like to put a slug in him my own self,' Etta said between her teeth.

Frank shook his head. 'We don't want any killings here on the ranch. You stay put, Etta. You go see the runt off, Lonny ...'

156

Once Dave Starr was sure he had not been followed by any suspicious-minded lawmen out of Mesquite, he took things more easily.

Soon after noon he found his way into Brownfield and partook of a good-sized meal whilst the steel-dust was being cared for.

Despite his size, Dave possessed that rare quality of being able to make himself inconspicuous. He always kept his hat well pulled down over his eyes and his whole figure appeared smaller and shorter as he leaned against walls and bar counters, rolling a quirly every so often.

It seemed he was able to keep his face partially averted from almost everyone, without evoking much curiosity or inviting suspicion. Such was the man whom Allan Pinkerton had selected for the almost impossible chore of breaking up the Sutter gang.

During the Civil War, Starr had worked closely with 'Major Allan', head of the Secret Service for the North. Now, at

Pinkerton's bidding, Dave had already covered hundreds of miles in his search for one of the first organized bands of outlaws in America.

He did not take long to size up Brownfield as a Southern stronghold. Some of these durn Southerners never did seem to realize that the war was over and done with.

He saw Shiro Calvin from a distance and rightly concluded, merely by looking at the lawman, that Calvin had probably ridden with some company or other of the Confederate cavalry.

By keeping his ears open and appearing to be deep in his own thoughts, Dave had not found it too difficult to pick up one or two snippets concerning Frank Sutter and his brothers. Enough at least to increase his suspicions of their guilt concerning the bank robbery and for him to learn that the Sutter boys were 'respectable ranchers over to the old Bennet spread.'

So far, news of the stage hold-up and the four killings had not apparently reached Brownfield. Even when it did,

Dave doubted very much whether it would make any difference. No-one would testify against their own kind; for in the eyes of most Southerners, all lawmen were Federals. They did not seem to realize that men like Sutter and his gang were the worst type of desperadoes—bushwhackers!

Again, it was not difficult to ascertain the location of the Bennet spread. And, once this was done, he set out from town, taking the narrower trails, thinking with a wry crooking of his lips how foolish men could be.

Here was he, a trusted Pinkerton operative, riding out to a hornets' nest with no other notion in his head than to try and do something about Etta Storm! He laughed aloud. He wasn't at all sure she was there, though everything pointed to it.

Every man had his weakness in one way or another, Starr thought. With some it was gold and with others it was drink or land or power or women.

There were other things too many to enumerate, but with Dave Starr it was

Etta Storm; her wild beauty and those shining blue eyes had been an image in his mind night and day since he had first seen her last Wednesday.

He knew he was a fool and there was even a fair chance he might be discovered and killed. Yet one sane thing he had done was to send a long wire in code to Chicago from the Telegraph Office in Mesquite.

Only Pinkerton's would be able to decipher it and it would give them all the knowledge and even the hunches that Dave possessed right now.

With the sun lowering towards the western rim, Dave watered his horse and sat on a boulder and lit a quirly and gazed around him at this sun-baked country and the sky above and wondered at the power Etta had over him that he was even prepared to take the chance of death.

At dusk, Dave rode on and at full dark saw the lamp-lit silhouette of a building and knew it for what it was.

He tied his mount to a sage clump,

well-shadowed, and went forward on foot until the sound of men's voices held him in his tracks.

He stood still and straight under a cottonwood not twenty yards from the house, seeing men move in front of the lighted windows, hearing the general bustle and activity that a cowpoke associates with a ranch, big or small.

Only once did Starr move and that was to place his hand on the butt of his gun as one of the gang rode up to the corral from the direction of the bawling cattle.

But all he did was to off-saddle, send his mount into the corral and make his own noisy way up the porch steps and into the house.

Dave could have used a drink or a smoke. Instead of which he just went on waiting, and at length his patience was rewarded ...

CHAPTER NINE

Moonlight on the Grass

Etta came down the veranda steps, lifting her face to the night breeze, remembering how she had performed just such an action the night she had ridden out from Buck Weidman's place.

Well, Lonny had sent the hateful Weidman scurrying away with a liberal dose of salt on his tail. She did not think that she had anything more to fear either from Buck or Cass.

She moved out and across the yard and paused near the cottonwood, and suddenly her mouth was covered and her body held as in a vice and she was being carried through brush and grass, further and further away from the house.

She was powerless to resist; it was difficult enough to breathe and only her eyes were free. Yet as she could not turn her head she was unable to obtain any clue as to who her kidnapper might be.

As to the ease with which he carried her, she could only think of Frank Sutter who lay wounded back there in the house. Even Lonny could not have held her as this man did, even if he had dared to try.

She tried to open her mouth to scream and only succeeded in biting his hand; but he seemed not to feel it.

Then, as suddenly as she had been whisked away from the ranch, she found herself on her feet once more, the man's arms still strongly around her. She saw then that he had brought her to beyond the grassy ridge, which meant that the ranch was out of sight a mile away.

She saw the horse tied to a clump of sage and then the hand came away from her mouth and she turned her head and looked into the shadowed face of Dave Starr.

She was a little scared, but fury at such treatment was the over-riding emotion and for a long moment it held her on the near brink of explosion.

Dave said: 'Don't scream, Etta. I give you my word that no harm'll come to you—'

'What are you tryin' to do, an' how come you knew—?' Her words came through clenched teeth and Dave could feel the soft yet rawhide strength of her as she struggled to free herself from his arm which still encircled her waist.

Swiftly he bent his head to hers and kissed her on the mouth. She summoned her reserves of strength with which to fight back but, once more, the startling suddenness of this man caught her unawares.

He stepped back, releasing her completely, and stood with his calm gaze on her face, upturned in the moonlight.

'I'm sorry,' he said at last. 'I hadn't any right to take such liberties. It's just that you're so all-fired lovely and I—well, I figgered—'

She looked at him with a puzzled expression in her dark-shadowed eyes. The fear and anger in her had all at once receded into the background.

She said in a husky voice: 'What's this all about, Dave Starr? Why did you come here and who are you? Don't tell me you're workin' for Buck Weidman—?' She took a step backward and clapped a hand to her gun-belt, only to discover that the holster was empty and that the Navy Colt hung loosely from Dave's left hand.

'So! You got my gun, Mister Starr! You're as full of tricks as a hound dog's full of fleas! But you still haven't told me anythin', have you?'

Dave built a quirly and lighted it with care. 'I'm not workin' for Weidman. Do you figger I'd take you back to a skunk like that?'

'How d'you know what he's like?'

Dave shrugged: 'I picked up a bit of gossip in Brownfield this afternoon. Seems like Weidman's bin out lookin' for his niece an' folks didn't give him much help. I even heard he used to whip you, Etta—'

'Then why don't you let me be now I finally gotten away from him an' that rotten son of his?'

'What you doin' here at the Lazy S, Etta; cookin' for this man Sutter?'

She regarded him through narrowed eyes. How much did this tough and handsome stranger know?

'Why not? Isn't it better'n bein' treated like a dog by your own kinsfolk?'

'Mebbe.' He drew on the quirly before continuing. 'You asked a whole heap o' questions just now, Etta, so I'll tell you what I can.

'I hit Mesquite a coupla weeks back; lookin' for grazing land. Figgered mebbe I'd buy a small spread or throw a few cattle on the open range an' start from scratch.

'Then Monday, as you know, the bank at Mesquite was robbed and Tuesday mornin' you rode in—'

'What do you mean by that?'

'Nothing at all. Just a plain statement of fact is all.' He got up, crushed out the stub of his quirly and stood close to the girl.

'I followed you, to Meeks' place, an' waited for you to come out.'

Etta stared at him with wide-open eyes,

unable to ask the questions that trembled on her lips and wondering how many more shocks were to come.

Dave smiled easily. 'Sure seemed a long time, but then I guess you and Meeks had plenty to talk about. I didn't know then, of course, that you'd run away and that a skunk of a man called Weidman had bin ill-treatin' you.'

Etta's breath came out of her mouth in a soft, enduring sigh. She found words at last. 'What did you do then?'

'What else but follow you out here, Etta, to the Lazy S. I figgered mebbe Meeks had given you some sort of introduction to this rancher called Sutter. I hung around, but as you didn't come out I concluded you'd hired yourself out—'

'That's exactly what I did, an' I still cain't understand what this is all about, Dave! Why pick me up like you was kidnappin' me an' bring me out here?' There was a wariness in her eyes now and Dave could sense that her whole body was as taut as a bow-string.

He said carefully: 'These Sutter brothers,

they aren't for you, Etta. Mebbe they are legitimate ranchers but there's more'n one man in Brownfield ready to hint that the Lazy S is bein' filled up with wet cattle—'

'Wet cattle?'

'Sure. Rustled stock.'

'What else they say in town about the Lazy S?'

Dave shrugged. 'I reckon Brownfield don't seem to mind much.'

He looked around over the moonlit scene. 'Most all o' this country represents the South—'

'An' you're a Yankee, ain't you, Dave? Why didn't I realize this before?'

'What difference does it make, Etta? The war's over and done with. We've got to start building up anew—'

'What exactly do you expect *me* to do about it?'

He could have crushed her in his arms, but he held himself back with the dismal remembrance of this morning, when she and the Sutter gang had robbed and killed on the stage road to Cottonwood Junction.

He said: 'Get out from the Lazy S before it's too late, Etta. Likely enough it's true there's stolen beef over there. Mebbe these men'll rob again an' mebbe there'll be killings!'

'If what you say is true; what you say is rumoured in town, then how come the law hasn't come visitin' us? And another thing, Dave. You still haven't told why you followed me around Mesquite an' then out here?'

'Haven't I? Well, let's say it's because you'd be better off mebbe with Weidman—'

'*Goddamit!*' she hissed. 'It's easy to talk, isn't it? Sure. Talk's cheap as dirt. As cheap an' as useless as Buck an' Cass Weidman theirselves!'

She swung away from him, opening her shirt and slipping it from her shoulders so that even in the uncertain light he could make out the dark scars across her back.

'Take a good look, Dave Starr, and see what Weidman's done to me over the past two-three years! You think I'd ever go back there? Why, I'd—'

'You'd rather kill than go back to Weidman, wouldn't you?' he asked softly.

'What do you mean? Why must you keep on talkin' in riddles?' the girl demanded as she pulled up the shirt and buttoned it to her neck.

'Hearing a vague rumour is one thing,' Dave answered, his voice rough with anger. 'Seeing those scars is a different thing. Why, I reckon if I was in your place, Etta, I might figger on killing the man myself rather than go back!'

'Sure. Then why bring me out here an' ask me—?'

He shook his head. 'Like I said, I didn't know it was as bad as that. But in any case I'm not askin' you to go back to Weidman; not now.'

Impulsively the girl placed her hands on his arms. 'Mebbe you have bin tryin' to help me, Dave. I don't know. As to any stolen cattle on the ranch, well, I wouldn't know about that either. Mebbe Mr Sutter *has* found a few strays and put his iron on them. Isn't that kinda thing being done almost every day? How else

170

is a man goin' to start buildin' anew, as you put it, with the dam' Federals havin' stripped the South bare?'

'You got a point there, Etty, but stock stealin' and mebbe even killing isn't goin' to help things—'

'What proof have you got, anyway, even if it's any concern of yours?'

He shook his head. 'I haven't any proof. What I'm concerned about is you gettin' mixed up with men like these an' mebbe startin' somethin' you cain't finish.'

'There you go, talkin' like a durned Easterner again! Don't you know that a woman on her own in the West is allus branded with the same mark?'

'Yeah. But mebbe I could fix somethin' for you. Some kind of job in Brownfield or Mesquite where you could be—'

'—A respected member of the community?' The faint smile on Etta's lips drew some of the sting from her words. Then she added: 'I gotta be goin' now, Dave. Mr Sutter'll be wonderin' where I am.'

'There is one solution,' Starr told her

in an odd voice. 'You could marry—someone.'

'Marry? You crazy or somethin'?'

Dave Starr nodded. He said in a sober tone: 'Sure I'm crazy; crazy as a loco'd steer. Crazy enough to be—' He broke off so abruptly that Etta looked up into his face as though she might find there the words he had left unspoken.

She felt strangely bewildered and for perhaps the first time in her life a feeling of yearning swept through her. Yet, uneasily, she still wondered how much this man knew about Frank and the boys and the part she herself was now playing.

Then Dave Starr's arms were around her and once more she felt his lips on hers; but this time it was he who drew away first as almost desperately he searched her upturned face.

She was beautiful, he thought, yet today she had made her most terrible mistake. Was it even now too late? he wondered. Was she to be branded henceforth and for the rest of her life, and become like the Sutter gang, killers and robbers to be

172

hunted down and killed?

He saw the scene of the stage hold-up as though it were reflected in the depths of her dark eyes. Yes, she had ridden with these men, but had her own gun fired any of the death shots? He knew he was playing with technicalities; the marks on her back bore evidence to the fact that there could have been little or no love shown her so far in life. Little wonder that she had run away from Weidman and an existence that must have been one of miserable humiliation.

'Dave! I gotta go now!' Her voice sounded harsh where before it had been soft and musical.

'You needn't go back, Etta; not if you were to marry me!'

She pulled away from him then and he made no attempt to hold her, and for a long moment she stood looking at him.

Then she took the gun from Dave's unresisting hand, turned and began walking back up the ridge where the waving grass was silver-tipped in the moonlight ...

Dave Starr rode slowly through the night,

his face etched into lines of bitter thoughtfulness.

He realized almost with dismay that there was no longer any doubt about his feelings towards the raven-haired girl. His proposal of marriage, curt and sudden as it was, had not been just a device to save Etta from the Sutter gang. He had meant it. Now, how was he going to hunt down these men, arrest or maybe even kill them, with Etta in their midst and participating perhaps in future robberies and killings?

There were other angles, too. Sooner or later, Sheriff Carter would want to know why he, Dave Starr, just hung around Mesquite without making a move to get a job or start a spread of his own. And there was Allan Pinkerton back in Chicago, employing him to bring in these men who had continued their looting and killing long after the war had finished.

Mesquite was still going full blast when Dave reached town.

Burr Parker was now back at the livery, so after Dave had stabled his horse he made for a restaurant and ate supper.

While his strong teeth chewed at the tough beef, his brain continued to gnaw at the problem which beset him. He needed help, but it was not so easy to get local peace-officers to see eye to eye with a Pinkerton man.

In the case of Shiro Calvin, his sympathies were obviously with Sutter's gang. They had all fought for the South and in their hearts they were still fighting all damned Yankees.

Carter was a Federal man and so were his two deputies; but if Dave put his cards on the table, he knew what would happen. Carter would organize a big posse to go after Frank Sutter and his boys and it would be a case of shoot first and ask questions after.

Dave couldn't see any posse men sticking their necks out and getting themselves killed just because some Pinkerton man had his sights lined on a lovely girl bandit.

Restless and for want of something better to do, Dave made his way to the Yellow Rose and called for a drink.

He stood at the crowded bar, resting

one elbow atop the polished surface and letting his gaze drift over the sea of shining faces. There were drovers, buyers, traders, percentage girls and even a few miners. But Dave's eyes were pinned to the face of a man he had not seen for two years.

It was a sun-burned, seamed face with crows' feet around the pale blue eyes and caliper lines deeply engraved on either side of the waterfall moustache.

He was seated at a table, drinking from a bottle, and he wore the same old alkali-covered fringed shirt, army trousers and moccasins. It was George Ridout, one-time trapper and, later on, scout to the 6th Illinois Cavalry.

Dave pushed his way through the roystering crowd, grasped the bottle just as Ridout was about to place it to his lips. In a flash, the scout's Bowie knife was out and men were edging away right and left, sending chairs sliding backwards as they moved clear.

Then Ridout's eyes gleamed and his knife was back at his belt and he was hugging Dave Starr like a bear ...

They sat at Ridout's table against the wall, remembering old times, and Dave said: 'What you doin' here, George?'

Ridout grinned. 'Same as before, Dave, only thar ain't much doin' at the moment around Fort Bliss.'

Dave nodded. The seed of an idea had begun to germinate in his mind.

'I've got a tough chore on, George; toughest I ever had, I reckon—'

'You mean you could use a leetle help?'

'You don't know what it is yet. Besides, if you're still scoutin' for the army—'

Ridout grinned. 'I'm Chief of Scouts at Fort Bliss, an' I ain't had any leave in a coon's age. This nigger's only gotta say the word. 'Sides which, I'd as lief walk out if I felt inclined. You got any trouble you wanta share, Davey, boy, you can count me in. What's the set-up?'

Starr lowered his voice; not that there was much chance of their conversation being overheard above the surrounding noise.

Briefly he told how he was working once again for Allan Pinkerton, trailing

177

the Sutter boys and their gang and Ridout remembered only too well.

'Reckon you cain't get much co-operation from the law hereabouts, huh?' the scout said. 'Not even if they are Federals.'

'It's not as simple as that,' Dave returned. 'Mebbe Sheriff Carter would co-operate if I asked him. But Sutter's got a girl with him now.'

Ridout slid his friend a calculating sideways glance. 'You got an interest; is that the way things lie?'

'You never did need a picture drawing, George, did you?'

The other grinned. 'I dunno. Thar's still one-two things I ain't yet got straight. You telling me Sutter's kidnapped this girl—?'

'No. She joined him because she was sick of bein' whipped an' kicked around like a dog by her own kinsfolk. That's why I figger she's not entirely to blame. By God, George, wouldn't you've done the same thing—if it was the only way—if you'd bin in her shoes?'

The scout nodded. 'Reckon I would,

an' I'm beginnin' to see the problem. We bring the law in on this, the girl's likely to be killed, or mebbe arrested, an' take the blame for what Frank an' his brothers has bin doin'!'

'That's the way I figger it, too.'

'Say. You musta talked with her, I reckon? Then don't she know or guess you're on to the Sutter outfit?'

Dave shook his head, explaining how he had met and tailed Etta Storm and their ensuing conversation.

'They're frontin' as respectable ranchers, near the town of Brownfield, south of here aways. I just seen Etta not more'n three hours back.

'But that's not all. You heard the bank was robbed—?'

'Sure. An' a coupla men killed. You ain't tellin' me Etta—?'

'No. But it was Sutter and his boys, of that I'm sure. And now—' Dave stopped and again Ridout gave his friend that shrewd, penetrating glance. He said softly: 'Thar's talk all over town about the Express stage bein' held up an' robbed early this

mawnin'. You thinkin' what I'm thinkin',
Dave?'

'I don't *think*. I know. I saw most of it
happen from a mile or so away.'

'So! It was Maury's ex-guerrillas fightin'
the war all over agin!'

'Yeah. That's bad enough in itself. But
you see, George, *Etta was along with
them!*' ...

CHAPTER TEN

A Piece of Calico

Two surprises were to confront Dave Starr
the following day at the inquest, and it was
Doc McCready, the coroner, who threw
the first bombshell.

'This court has been convened,' Mc-
Cready said, 'to enquire into the deaths
of Jim Drake and George Bix, driver and
shot-gun guard respectively of the stage
held up and robbed yesterday morning.

'The third man was special messenger Ed Coles. At the moment, Henry Forrest is still alive, but as he is unconscious and in a critical condition, he obviously cannot give evidence.'

Sheriff Carter got to his feet and McCready nodded towards him.

'Would it help any, doc, if this court was adjourned until—'

McCready shook his head. 'In my opinion, it is unlikely that Mr Forrest will live. In any case it might be weeks or even months before he could give evidence. He has lost more blood than any man should and still go on living.

'Now, Sheriff Carter. Since you are already standing, perhaps you would tell the court what you know.'

But Carter could tell little enough. The only thing of interest was when he hinted at the identity of the gang.

'Can you tell this court who the road-agents were, Sheriff? Or who *any* of them were?'

Carter shook his head. 'It's only a hunch, sir. I guess I got no right to be namin' names without a shred of evidence.'

The coroner nodded and then called Art Black, who told his story much as he had done in the sheriff's office the previous day.

Dave and Ridout sat in the tightly packed court house, listening to the proceedings carefully. The two things that had taken Dave Starr by surprise were, firstly, the fact that Forrest was still alive; and secondly that Carter had hinted that he knew or had at least a suspicion as to who the road-agents were. It looked as though Carter *might* know something about the Sutter gang after all.

Dave shuddered at the thought that the sheriff might go off half-cocked and do something plumb foolish like swooping down on the Lazy S with a bunch of trigger-happy posse men ...

Meeks was called next and the cringing little man merely corroborated Art Black's statement regarding the reasons for the precaution which had been taken.

Meeks stuck to his story about the

warning note being pushed through his door and Dave knew then, without a doubt, what had taken place at Meeks' cottage the night he had followed Etta.

A stir ran round the assembly as Dave Starr was called to give his evidence as the only one present who had actually witnessed the hold-up.

'Please tell the court in your own words, exactly what happened yesterday morning, Mr Starr, from the time you rode out of town.'

Dave stood up and nodded. He said; 'Like I told the sheriff, sir, I was fixin' to ride into Brownfield.'

'Any special reason?'

Dave shrugged slightly. 'I heard there was a spread west aways. Pothook's the brand, run by a man called Jason or Jackson—'

'That's right,' McCready affirmed. 'In fact it's a Mr Jaxson who runs the Pothook Ranch.'

'Sure. Well, I thought mebbe he might use another rider, an' I figgered on makin' an early start.'

'Go on, Mr Starr.'

'I don't know this country well, so I decided to follow the stage road, having bin told there was a fork road to Brownfield some eight-ten miles from here.'

The coroner nodded and Dave continued. He said: 'The stage overtook me after about half an hour on account I was ridin' slow an' easy. Then, later on, I heard the sound of guns—'

'You say, "later on", Mr Starr, but have you in fact any idea how long it was from the time the stage passed you to the moment you heard the sounds of firing?'

'Mebbe an hour. I wasn't payin' much heed to time.'

'What did you do next?'

Dave lifted his broad shoulders in an almost weary gesture. 'I spurred forward till I reached a part of the road that rises to form a low ridge. The firing was still goin' on so I took to the brush at the roadside.'

'You could then see clearly down the road without you yourself being seen, is that it?'

'Yes, sir. I'd figgered that if the stage was bein' attacked, then likely there wasn't much I could do on my own.'

'You actually saw the stage being attacked?'

Dave nodded. 'I was about a mile away but I could see a bunch of riders wheelin' about in the dust. The stage wasn't movin' then—'

'Did you tell Sheriff Carter and Mr Black, here, that you used a telescope?'

'I sure did, sir. But even with a glass, it wasn't easy to pick out anything in partic'lar. The men was all ridin' dark horses an' had their faces covered. By this time, the shootin' was over, but one of the men blew the lock off the strong box.'

'What then?'

Dave gave a meagre smile. 'They didn't waste any time transferring the money—'

'How did you know it was money if you couldn't see any details?' McCready asked.

Dave said tightly: 'I ridden shot-gun guard in my time an' I ain't ever seen road-agents hold up a stage for grass-seed!'

A ripple of laughter ran around the court room and the coroner flushed and brought down his gavel for silence.

'At least I saw what looked like a strong box,' Dave went on quickly, 'so I figgered they was takin' some kinda pay-roll or gold shipment. Sure enough, soon as they were gone, and I was able to ride up, there was the box with the lock blown off, and—'

'What else do you remember seeing, particularly in those first few moments?'

'The two lead horses had bin shot dead to halt the coach. The driver had fallen to the ground with a bullet in his chest and the guard was sprawled along the seat with a slug in his head.'

'And then?'

'I opened the nearside door of the coach an' a man fell out. It looked like he was dead. He was still holdin' a Colt's gun but he was shot up bad an' pale lookin'—I—I guess I just figgered he couldn't be still alive.'

'That's understandable,' agreed Mc-Cready. 'I thought the same thing yesterday at first glance.'

'I sure am glad about Forrest, sir,' Dave said soberly. 'I mean that he's not dead—'

'And what about the other messenger, Ed Coles?'

'He was lyin' on the floor of the coach. If you saw him when I brought the stage back—'

'Yes, yes. There could be no doubt about *his* condition.'

'Well, I reckon there isn't much else to tell. I cut the team free and tooled the coach back here, leavin' it with Mr Black an' the sheriff.'

'This court,' McCready said, 'acknowledges the fact that no one man could have done more than you did, Mr Starr. It expresses its admiration for your prompt action in driving the stage coach back. If Mr Forrest lives, it will be largely thanks to your efforts.'

The verdict was a foregone conclusion. McCready could only rule that the three men had been killed and the fourth severely wounded, by unknown robbers. A rider was added that another inquest would take place if Forrest died, but that a special inquiry would be called for, should Henry Forrest recover sufficiently to tell his story ...

Over a meal in one of Mesquite's smaller restaurants, Ridout and Dave Starr began discussing the situation.

'What you gonna do now, Dave? How kin you help this kitten without gettin' yoreself plumb kilt or somethin'?'

'I ain't sure yet, George. First off, I figger we ought to quit Mesquite an' hang around Brownfield for a while. Trouble is, I ain't sure whether Carter's got anythin' up his sleeve—'

'You mean he's already figgerin' it was the Sutter gang?'

Dave nodded. 'You heard how he hinted that he knew—or had suspicions—who it was.'

'Then why in tarnation didn't that coon McCready make him spit it out?'

'He couldn't, George. It was a coroner's court, not a court of law, and Carter told all he *knew*. He couldn't be forced to come out with guesses.'

'All right. Then what we gonna do? Mebbe we could attack this Lazy S place our own selves and—'

'It wouldn't work, I reckon, an' it'd be too risky. But mebbe we could bait a trap for the gang; spread some rumour of a stage shipment sufficiently big and easy to whet their appetites.'

'So?'

Dave leaned forward across the table. 'If we could do that, George, an' if Etta figgered on stayin' put at the ranch—'

'You mean we could snatch her while most of Sutter an' his boys is out on the raid?'

'Yeah. But there's one-two snags. I saw Frank Sutter bein' helped away on his horse. I'm sure it was him an' I reckon mebbe he was bad hurt.'

'Then they won't be pullin' any more raids 'till Sutter's fit again?'

'Mebbe. Mebbe not. An' mebbe Etta'll be stayin' behind to nurse him.'

Ridout pulled at his whiskers thoughtfully. 'Seems to me, Dave, thar's too many ifs and buts. An' supposin' we could pull sech a trick an' get the kitten away. Wal, then. How you gonna stand if the gang splits up an' takes for the brush?'

'Sure. I'm thinkin' about that, too. I reckon you must figger I'm seven kinds of a fool an' likely you'd be right at that!'

Ridout's blue eyes took on a misty, faraway look. 'I mind the time way back when I took a real shine to a Blackfoot kitten. 'Twas in the Three Forks country an' me an' three others was riskin' our hair fer beaver. Did I ever tell you, Dave?'

Starr smiled. 'No. But I reckon you as likely took on the whole Blackfoot nation if you wanted this girl.'

Ridout grinned, obviously pleased by the compliment. 'Trouble was, *she* was the one. Crept outa her daddy's lodge one night an' rode two hull days an' nights to find me!'

'So?'

Ridout emptied his glass and shrugged. 'The others told me to take the girl an' high-tail it fer the valleys. They wasn't gonna risk their hair fer no Blackfoot wench as had taken a shine to me!'

'So they walked out on you?'

Ridout's brows went up in surprise. 'Why shouldn't they? They was the smart niggers, this chile the fool, Dave, jest like you.'

'All right. What happened?'

'What else but I upped an' rode back with her to her daddy's lodge an' her close up behind me on the hoss on account she'd ridden her own pony plumb into the ground.'

'I sure cain't understand why they didn't cut you up for supper, George.'

'They dam' near did, only Runnin' Stream—that was her English name—told her paw what had happened an' added a few choice things about me. Consequence was, he sent me off with a spare cayuse loaded with plews.'

'But you never saw the girl again?'

Ridout's face went dead looking.

He said softly: 'I was up thar when the smallpox struck. I found Runnin' Stream in a deserted village. She an' a brave an' a papoose was all lyin' daid in an empty *tipi*. I buried all three of 'em together an' got drunk on Taos Lightnin' fer nigh on a month.'

Dave didn't know what to say, so he replenished the glasses.

'Funny thing was,' Ridout rumbled, 'I found the three niggers I'd bin with the fust time, some ways along the trail. They, too, was daid, which jest goes to show somethin' or other, don't et, Dave?'

'Mebbeso. But you were a free trapper, George. You had a right to take all the fool risks you wanted. You didn't work for a Company an' swear to keep certain articles of faith.'

'Listen,' Ridout hissed. 'I cain't say as I hold with cold-blooded murder, though I killed a passel o' two-legged skunks in my time. But, we ain't certain sure that the kitten's done any killin' an' if she—'

'She was with the killers, George, that's for sure, whatever else, an' she had a big hand in that stage robbery an' I'm pretty certain that she helped rob the bank as well—'

'No jury out here's gonna convict a

purty young girl like that! Wasn't she druv to it? Wasn't she whipped an' beaten like a cur dog? An'—'

'All right! So mebbe there's still a chance. But she's made up her mind to stay with Sutter. There'll be other times, other robberies an' killin's an' mebbe Etta'll be killed or do some her own self. How we gonna stop it happenin', George?'

Ridout cut a thin slice of tobacco and popped it in his mouth. He chewed in thoughtful silence for a long time.

'Wal, now,' he said presently. ''Pears like to me we got several things to do right now. Fust off, I'll fix me some leave, then we'll high-tail towards Brownfield.'

'What do you mean, "towards Brownfield"?'

Ridout grinned. 'We's conspicuous enough here in Mesquite. In Brownfield we'd stick out like a coupla sore thumbs.

'Now I know the Bennet spread an' I mind an old cabin that usta be used afore the river changed course.'

'You mean it's deserted now?'

The other nodded. ''Bout six months back I hadta trail an enlisted man who'd deserted from the fort an' taken a few pokes o' gold with him. The fust night out I holed up in thet cabin. I tell you, Dave, 'tis an ideal spot an' I reckon no-one goes that way more'n is necessary.'

'But you say the river's gone?'

'Sure. But there's a pump near the shack an' it's still workin'. Judgin' by the water it must go down mighty deep.'

Inconsequentially, Dave asked: 'What happened about the trooper you was tailin'?'

'Oh. I caught up with him a coupla days later. He saw me comin' an' sent a slug clean through my shoulder. Then he took to his heels.'

'You mean you lost him?'

Ridout stared in genuine surprise.

'Lost him? 'Course not. I pinned him a'tween the shoulder blades with Nancy here!' He patted the Bowie knife nestling in the ornate leather scabbard at his belt ...

Ridout was back from Fort Bliss inside of three hours and found Dave leaning against a roof post near the Yellow Rose.

'You-all set, Dave?'

The detective nodded, but a furrow lay between his black brows.

'I bin thinkin' about the law here, George—'

'So've I. Mebbe one of us'll haveta come back an' watch Carter an' his sidekicks, but meanwhile I gotta show you that place.'

Dave laid his gaze on the pack horse that Ridout was trailing and the latter grinned widely. 'Sure. Got it all here; everythin' we's likely to need.'

Starr nodded, untied his mount from the nearby hitch rack and swung up.

The two men made their unhurried way from town, with no more than a passing glance from the few folk in the near vicinity.

The afternoon sun beat down from a brassy sky. Dave shifted now and again in the saddle as though this small action might in some way cool his body. Ridout led the way, a half length ahead, nosing out the trail. He sat slumped in the saddle, like an Injun, but there wasn't a durn thing he missed, either on the ground or on the distant waving grass.

He smelt no danger. It was in the very roots of his being to go slow and careful. Sometimes, a man had to move like greased lightning; but mostly it was a case of slow and sure. It had paid dividends in the past, and that was how Ridout came to see the insignificant and almost invisible speck of white at the base of a sage bush.

Leisurely he slid from leather and threw a rein into Dave's outstretched hand. He moved across the hard, tufted grass which sprang from the alkali strewn ground and walked a distance of a dozen yards or more.

Dave, waiting, saw him stoop and pick up something white; a small square of calico, maybe.

Ridout straightened up. 'Hoss tracks along here, Dave. Cain't see 'em from where we was.'

'How fresh?'

The scout scratched his head and spat. 'Coupla hours, mebbe. No more'n three, I'd say.'

Dave quickly secured the horses and walked over to where Ridout was standing. He took the white square from the scout's hand, recognizing it as a woman's handkerchief. Not a fine cambric such as a well-to-do lady might own, but a hand-embroidered square made more for use than for any decorative purpose. It was almost childishly hemmed, and then Dave drew in his breath as he saw the small initials laboriously embroidered in one corner. He looked up and found the scout's sober blue gaze pinned on him.

'"E.S.",' Dave said slowly. 'I reckon I never did tell you Etta's other name was Storm.'

Ridout shrugged. 'Could mean anythin'. Could even've bin planted here. But if the kitten dropped it her own self by accident, it don't mean nothin' more than she's ridden by here, alone, purty recent.'

Dave nodded. 'Sure. But it's not the way I'd 've figgered it, somehow; not with Frank Sutter shot up. What else do them tracks tell you?'

The scout laid his gaze on the rolling, sage dotted grass ahead as though he had already extracted every particle of knowledge from the sign at his feet.

'Light tracks, Dave, an' spread wide. The hoss was travellin' some. Imprints ain't too deep, like you can see. No doubt the rider was a girl. Light as a passel o' tumbleweed.'

'Well, what the hell am I gettin' steamed up for, George? Tell me that!'

Ridout said: 'You figgered thet kitten'd stay put on account o' Sutter bein' wounded. Now she's already sashayin' around, an' what's she doin' usin' an old Injun trail like this?'

'What d'you mean?'

'We's headin' fer the cabin, Dave. But the ole Bennet buildin's is well nigh due south from here. If the kitten was ridin' into Mesquite or Brownfield either, she wouldn't hardly come this way. Is this what's puzzlin' you, Davey?'

Starr pushed back his hat and wiped sweat from his face. 'I dunno; it just don't seem to make a right pattern. Any other town hereabouts she could 'a' bin headin' fer?'

'Yeah, I guess. Away back was a fork; mebbe you saw it, but it ain't used in a coon's age. Leads to a farming town called Signal. Mebbe she was goin' there?'

Dave shrugged. 'You still got eyes like a hawk, George. Ain't no-one else would've spotted this handkerchief, but where's it get us? C'mon, let's ride.'

They continued onwards into more rocky country, the waving grass was now falling away on their right flank.

A small stand of cottonwoods lay ahead, still drawing life and moisture from deep down, despite the almost arid soil. They crossed the rock-strewn bed of the dried-up water course and came within sight of the derelict cabin a mile or so away.

The building, if such it could be called, was a broken down one-roomed affair with four bunks, a rickety table and an ancient rusted stove. Everything was covered by a shroud of yellow dust.

But, like Ridout had said, the pump, miraculously, still worked and the water, when it eventually came through, was as cool and refreshing as a mountain stream.

Dave loosened the surcingle and rubbed down his mount, noting almost subconsciously that the animal was in good shape. He straightened up and walked over to where Ridout was unloading the supplies.

'George,' he said quietly, 'I gotta hit that trail for Signal.'

'But it ain't reasonable—'

'I know,' Dave said. 'Feelings seldom are reasonable. You wait for me here?'

The grizzled old scout nodded. 'If that's the way you want it, Dave.'

CHAPTER ELEVEN

Etta Goes It Alone

Ever since she had left Dave Starr standing there in the moonlight, Etta's mind had been flooded with doubts and misgivings which she could not entirely subdue.

She returned to the ranch house and was hauled up abruptly by Lonny's voice.

'That you, Etta? Where in hades you bin? Frank's bin askin' for you—'

She came on then, quickly, and swept past Lonny, leaving him wide-eyed with surprise and a little angry at her downright unfriendly attitude.

She went through the living room, conscious of the men's eyes on her and opened the door at the far end.

Frank was sitting up in bed, his arm in a black sling. A few feet away, Doc was reading a paper, and across the room

Jim Sutter squatted on the floor, cleaning his gun.

'Hallo, Etty. Where you bin?'

'Just takin' some air, is all. How's the shoulder feelin', Frank?'

'Not too bad, but I'm as weak as a kitten when it comes to standin' on my legs.'

''Course you are,' Doc said sourly. 'You lost a deal of blood—'

'What you wanta see me about, Frank; anythin' in particular?'

'Just wanted to see you, I reckon, Etty, an' let you know I'm not bein' entirely idle.'

'What he means,' Jim said, grinning, 'is he's plannin' some raid for us-all, just in case we start gettin' bored!'

'The sooner the better, far as I'm concerned,' Etta said with some vehemence. 'Frank! I gotta have some decent clothes. I ain't walkin' around any longer in this hand-me-down nester rig-out!'

Frank's blue eyes opened a trifle wider. 'Sure. We'll see about it some time—'

'Some time ain't good enough, Frank! This mornin' I helped you lift ten thousand

202

bucks. I guess some o' that *dinero* belongs to me, don't it?'

'You'll get your cut, Etta,' Dufresne said mildly. 'What you gettin' steamed up about?'

'She's right, Abe, an' you know it,' Frank said quickly. He didn't want any trouble with this wild young thing, particularly as she had so soon proved herself up to the hilt. Frank Sutter judged that the time had come to show Etta that her qualities were fully appreciated.

'Doc'll give you a coupla hundred dollars, Etta,' he said slowly. 'But there's one condition.'

'Oh? So there's a catch?'

'No catch at all. Just that I ain't havin' you ride into Mesquite or Brownfield is all. Someone might stop you an' start askin' you questions—'

'But—'

'Wait till I've finished! There's a small town called Signal not far off. You can get most anything there you'll want. Mebbe you know, anyway?'

Etta nodded. 'I bin there a coupla times;

once with Weidman an' once with Cass, but that was more'n a year ago. Ain't anyone there would know me now!'

'Good. When you wanta go?'

'Tomorrow, for sure; mebbe around noon is best.'

'All right. But I don't want you cuttin' across the Mesquite or Brownfield trails—'

'Don't worry. There's an old Injun path north from here aways. Scarce anyone ever uses it and it goes through brush and rock, most of the way to Signal ...'

This morning, Etta felt elated at the prospect which lay before her. The day was not so hot, and a soft wind had sprung up, laying itself over this oven-hot land like a cool breath upon parched lips.

Lonny gave her a long, meditative glance as she saddled up and rode her mount from the pole corral. It was as though he were trying to find some fault, some edge which he could twist and turn against her. But she was careful; remembering to close and fasten the corral gate. Inwardly she was as wary as a stalking catamount as

204

she neck-reined the horse and rode off at an easy pace.

Once clear of the ranch, she extended the animal's gait to a long, mile-eating lope and felt a surge of something like happiness.

Frank had kept his word. Frank trusted her, even if Lonny did not. She had plenty of *dinero* in her pockets and was riding free as the air for the first time in her life.

Vaguely she realized that some kind of metamorphosis had taken place within her. She could scarcely understand that so short a time back she had cowered under Weidman's whip and had so often cried herself to sleep.

Now, everything was vastly changed. Now, she was getting a chance to get her own back on the world at large.

She thought ahead to the time when her name would be on people's lips, in much the same way as the names of Frank and his men were uttered, softly and with respect, back in Missouri.

She could understand clearly now why the Sutter boys were killers and robbers;

they had no choice any more than she herself. It was as simple as that.

Despite such fanciful thoughts, there was an inherent shrewdness in Etta Storm that prompted her to watch the country ahead. She even turned in the saddle on two separate occasions and surveyed her back trail with calculating care. Satisfied that she was not being followed, she urged her mount along the part-sheltered fork leading to Signal.

A half-mile or so from the edge of town, Etta dismounted and knelt down and faintly smeared her hands and face with trail-dust.

Then she caught at her black hair and pushed it up underneath the crown of her stetson, afterwards shrugging into the brush jacket which had been tied to the saddle.

She did not expect to be taken for a man, but at any rate she was now sufficiently inconspicuous to pass as some nester's daughter.

At this time of day with the sun

overhead, Signal's boardwalks were well nigh deserted. One or two riders ambled their mounts along the dusty street and a ranch wagon turned on to Main and pulled to a stop outside a hardware store.

Etta rode slowly, her eyes under the pulled down hat darting every which way. She wanted to size up this town before she took any kind of action, for, at the back of her mind, an idea had begun to form which for a while caused her heart to pound like a trip-hammer.

She found what she was looking for, several blocks down Main. The sign over the store said: *'Swayle's Emporium'* and in smaller lettering: *'If we haven't got it, we'll get it!'*

That sounded promising, Etta thought, but she neither dismounted nor even stopped. Instead she continued on until she came to the last intersection. She turned right and made her way past a livery and blacksmith shop, a harness shop and one-two shacks. She turned right again, passing a saloon and a honky-tonk, outside of which a girl in a near topless red dress stared blankly before her on to the sunlit street.

Etta completed her circuit and only dismounted when she was once more outside the hardware store. The ranch wagon was just moving away and the driver, an old cowhand by his appearance, spared Etta no more than a rheumy-eyed glance before tooling his wagon and team down-street.

Inside the store, amongst a heterogenous collection of farm and ranch implements, stoves and such like, Etta found a fair selection of hand guns and carbeens.

Jeff Baxter, looking over the top of his spectacles, was mildly surprised to realize that his customer was a woman—well, a girl, perhaps. He was somewhat more surprised when she asked to examine a tray of revolvers.

Etta picked up a .36 Navy Colt, hefting it in her hand, balancing it and finally cocking and triggering the empty gun.

'I want a two-holstered belt to go with that, Mister!'

Baxter wondered why this ill-dressed

nester girl had not even bothered to ask the price, but he kept his mouth shut and began rummaging around in a drawer, producing several belts, none of which satisfied his strange customer.

Finally Jeff Baxter produced the very thing, and had he been able to see the girl's eyes properly he would have been astonished at the gleam in their lovely blue depths.

'This is the very latest, Miss. Ain't many like it with them cartridge loops half-ways around.'

'Sure. Give it to me!'

She unbuckled her own belt and holster after withdrawing the gun. Then she fastened the twin-holstered belt around her hips.

'It needs a hole here,' she said, taking the belt off and indicating the exact spot with her finger.

Old Man Baxter nodded, found an awl and proceeded to make a new hole. 'Gun's seventy-five dollars, Miss, an' the belt's thirty—' He paused purposely, half expecting the girl to cry off. Instead, she dived a hand inside her brush jacket and produced a handful of coins and notes. She counted out one hundred and twenty-five dollars. She said coolly: 'This oughta take care of things. Fill up the belt with spare loads!'

Baxter stared hard, but his eyesight was not all that good and the girl's face was still part-shadowed by the brim of her hat. But at least the hardware merchant knew good money when he saw it and he moved quickly to finish transacting the best piece of business he had done in days ...

Etta's next call was at Swayle's Emporium and here she gazed around her in fascinated wonder at the surprising array of household goods of every description.

A young man came forward, his pimply face flushing slightly as Etta slipped off her brush jacket.

'I want a complete rig-out,' Etta told him, 'an' that means a ridin' skirt an' half boots, spurs, a blouse an'—an' everything.'

'I—I ain't sure we got—' The youth was obviously flummoxed by Etta's figure, by her forthright attitude and by the very nature of her request.

'Listen,' she said softly. 'You got a sign on the window that says you either got it else you get it! What's it to be? You tellin' me you ain't got any such things in your store?'

With an effort, the youth pulled himself together. 'We did have a ridin' skirt ordered special for a rancher's daughter. She never did collect it as I remember, Miss. Lemme see now. Ah, yes! I reckon I know where it was put.' He moved towards a drawer and then turned, his face wearing an anxious expression. 'I just remembered—no offence, Miss—but this was a special order an'—'

'—An' it cost a lot of *dinero?*' Etta sneered. 'Well, here's a hun'ed bucks for a start off! Now get me the best dam' clothes you got in this store!'

The boy nearly fell over himself in his eagerness to put up the order. Whoever this girl was, she was not short on money and old Swayle would be mad as hell if he lost or displeased a customer who laid cash on the line just like thumbing peas from a pod!

In five minutes, Andy Summers had found a fine grey woollen shirt and hat, a pair of hand-tooled Justin boots and spurs; a sleeveless heavily embroidered bolero and the riding skirt.

'You got some place I can try these on, Mister?'

Andy nodded. 'Sure. That store room yonder'll be all right. I—I'll see no-one disturbs you, Miss.'

For the first time he saw her eyes as she flashed him a quick, sideways glance. He had never seen such eyes in all his life; nor had a girl ever looked at him quite like that before.

Maybe he was imagining things, he thought, as he hurried forward to open the door and lay the clothes inside on a box.

He stood by the counter in a dream, unaware of the passage of time. It seemed only seconds later that the door swung open and she stood there like some magnificent queen of the prairie.

The dun-coloured stetson was pulled forward, but her ink-black hair hung loose to the shoulders of her shirt and gaily-decorated bolero. The divided, fringed skirt and hand-tooled boots fitted like a glove, and over all the two-gun belt nestled low around her hips.

Andy Summers was sure that he had never seen anything quite so magnificent in all his life. He would gladly have laid down and allowed this girl to walk right over him.

As for Etta, she was on fire with the thrill of these splendid clothes and the anticipation of what she was about to do.

Even with the money she had taken from Weidman, this spending spree would just about clean her out. But she could have laughed out loud at such a realization, for all she had to do now was take whatever she wanted.

She might well have robbed the store there and then and likely the pimply youth would have been incapable of making a move to stop her.

But she came forward, planked the

213

money down and asked for a gunny sack.

As in a dream, Andy Summers handed her an empty sack and still stood there, transfixed, even after she had gone and the sound of hoof-beats had diminished along the street ...

Etta dismounted outside the bank, leaving her horse loosely tied. In a moment she was within the shadows of the roofed-in boardwalk and entering the bank itself.

The teller, a grey-haired inoffensive little man, was busy counting out money and placing it in stacks. When he finally looked up he found himself staring straight down the barrel of a cocked gun, held coolly and firmly by a picturesquely dressed person whose face was half covered by a red bandanna and whose eyes were shadowed by a brand new, wide-brimmed hat.

'Fill this up!' Etta hissed, placing the gunny-sack on the counter, 'an' be dam' quick about it!' ...

Several times Dave Starr reined in on the brush-fringed fork trail to Signal and gazed down at the faint tracks of Etta's mount.

There was no doubt about it; they were identical to the sign Ridout had cut along the old Indian trail. Etta was in Signal for sure, and Dave wondered whether his hunch would pay off.

He shook his head. He would far sooner be wrong about this whole thing. For if Etta *was* trying to pull something on her own, then once again there was the chance that someone might be killed or seriously wounded.

Dave tried to consider what he would do if he had all the proof he needed about the Sutter gang. Would he call in Sheriff Carter and try to capture the whole caboodle, irrespective of whether Etta was with them?

He did not know; in any case, even though he had witnessed the stage robbery, that in itself was not evidence enough to convict Sutter and his men. They had all been masked for a start off and Dave did not doubt that they could furnish a perfect alibi and successfully protest that they were legitimate ranchers and not road-agents. No jury, Federal or otherwise, would take the word of one stranger against a 'respectable' rancher and his hands.

Maybe Carter had a shrewd idea that the Sutters were ex-Confederates turned outlaw; but an idea wasn't good enough. Whichever way you looked at it, you could do nothing without proof, unless you took the law into your own hands and faced the consequences of so rash an action.

Dave touched spurs to his mount and suddenly left the trail, striking cross-country towards a formation of rocks which he judged could not be far distant from town.

He hit the talus slopes and put the steel-dust to a series of narrow, ascending paths. Once he glimpsed the near buildings of Signal, visible between two outcroppings, and found that he was even closer in to town than he had expected.

Half-way up, a flat, mesa-like rock part-covered by boulders presented itself as the ideal place.

Dave slid from leather, tied his mount to a piñon bush and edged his way forward almost to the brink of the mesa rock. He was scarcely surprised to realize that the whole rock formation over-hung part of the town, giving him a grandstand aerial view of things.

It was better still when he placed the glass to his eye. He could almost see the expressions on the faces of one or two townsfolk as they leisured their way from the shaded boardwalks across the sun-drenched street.

He heard a shot, sharp and clear, and it came with a suddenness that he could not have anticipated.

He cast one quick glance back at his horse, making sure the animal was safely nearby, and the steel-dust threw up its head and nickered shrilly.

Dave's eyes turned back on the street as he saw a brilliantly clad figure run from the sidewalk and leap into the saddle of a waiting horse.

For a moment he thought it was some gaily dressed *vaquero* and then he saw the fringed skirt flying in the breeze as its owner spurred her mount away, just as another shot rang out along the street.

Quickly, Starr put the glass to his eye, bringing the racing figure unmistakeably clear and near. Then, in the twinkling of an eye, horse and rider had disappeared into the shadows of a side street, but not before Dave had noted the bulging gunny sack which Etta somehow contrived to hold firmly across the saddle horn.

The idea that Etta might have come here merely to buy herself a rig-out now hit Dave for the first time. He realized, grimly, that if such a commonplace explanation had occurred to him before he wouldn't be here at all, watching yet another robbery in which the girl had taken part.

Only this time there was a big difference. So far as he could see, Etta had done this thing on her own. All the way there had only been the single set of tracks; unless she was going to make rendezvous with some of Sutter's boys later on ...

From his eyrie, Dave could see at least half of the town and much of the brush-stippled, undulating country beyond.

On the street itself, confusion reigned

as folk tumbled from buildings and raised their voices in a babble of indignant questions, and from out the bank a shirt-sleeved oldster staggered, clutching a blood-stained arm.

Even from that distance, Dave heard a man's voice lift and say: 'The bank's bin robbed! You all right, Mr Dalston?'

The teller's voice came back, faint, yet clear enough for Dave. 'Sure. Ain't only a flesh wound. Where's Marshal Wilcox! Ain't someone goin' to ride out after that bandit?'

Dave let go his breath in a juddering sigh. *Thank God Etta had not killed!* She could not have done. Only the one shot had been fired at first and the teller was obviously not seriously wounded. The second shot had been fired *at* Etta, by someone on the street.

Dave put his glass to the country beyond as he caught a flash of movement. She came near again under the powerful lens, even though she appeared to be sweeping round in a wide circle some three miles yonder.

He saw then what she had in mind. She had left town by a certain route and the posse, if any, would give chase in that direction. But even now Etta was curving round, riding like the wind and headed back towards the fork trail over which both she and Dave had travelled!

CHAPTER TWELVE

Dave Ropes a Maverick

He remained for a while, hunkered down amongst the hot yellow rocks, thinking hard and only vaguely aware that on Signal's Main Street order was slowly beginning to emerge from that first confusion and shock.

The damned little maverick! he swore to himself. *What in heaven's name had possessed her?*

Even now, Dave Starr was not at all sure why he had come thus far, following Etta's trail to town; except that some instinct, some vague fear, perhaps, had driven him in the hope that he might avert disaster if it should come.

Well, it had come, yet it was not altogether quite so bad as it might have been. So far as Dave knew, Etta's hands were still clean of blood and, somehow or another, the stolen money must be returned to its rightful owners.

This was strictly not Dave's chore; yet it was one he had taken upon himself and one he was going to attempt despite the odds. But how?

A moment ago he had called her 'a damned little maverick' and the thought recurred to him and he smiled grimly. How else did a man deal with an old mossyhorn or a wild young maverick, except to rope and hog-tie it and clap his brand on?

The time for branding had not yet come—if it ever did—but the craziest longhorn was helpless once it had been thrown and tied, and Dave smiled again, despite the deep concern within him, and laid his gaze ahead and saw her for a moment flashing through a sparse stand of cottonwoods not much more than a mile away.

The little fool, to have robbed a bank in a rig-out unique enough to blazen her description throughout the country!

Cursing softly, Dave rose to his feet, untied his mount and went into the saddle.

He began to descend the rocky paths, veering as much as possible towards a rock-strewn talus slope that fell away almost to the very edge of the trail itself.

No sooner had he reached his objective, than he hid the steel-dust amongst the bigger boulders and took the *reata* from his saddle horn.

Holding the rawhide rope in his right hand, he moved as near to the edge of the trail as he dared, taking up a good position behind a scattering of rocks and brush.

He heard the soft drum of hoof-beats as horse and rider approached the trail from across the undulating grass to the north-east.

She was easing up now and Dave let

out a sigh of relief that, even in her crazy mood, Etta had sense enough not to flog her horse to death, nor to call attention by throwing up noise and dust like signposts in her wake.

His eyes were on the bend in the hard-packed road, and suddenly she appeared and hauled up and remained a while looking back.

Apparently satisfied, she tied the top of the bulging gunny sack with a length of rawhide and urged her mount forward at an easy canter.

Dave had the noose in his hand with the remainder of the *reata* loosely coiled. He stood poised and calm, confident that his *vaquero* rope trick would succeed.

Etta came on until she was abreast the rocks behind which Starr stood.

He risked a quick look and saw that she was almost past his hiding place. In another five seconds she would be beyond the range of his rope.

He made his throw, watching the rawhide snake through the air, the noose settling around Etta's shoulders and breasts even before she was aware of what was happening. Then, deliberately, Dave tightened his hold, jerking the *reata* hard so that the noose contracted cruelly and at the same time dragged the now struggling girl from the saddle.

In those first brief moments, when the shock of Etta's body hitting the ground held her still, Dave leaped forward, falling on the half-dazed girl and turning her over and placing his knee in the small of her back.

In a second he had whisked her own red bandanna up over her eyes, tightening the knot at the back of her head.

Though the breath had been knocked out of her for a few moments, Etta now began struggling and fighting like a wild-cat. But Dave knew what he was doing and held her in a vice-like grip as he turned her over, half raised her head and shoulders and clipped her hard on the jaw.

Etta's head jerked back and her body went slack, and quickly Dave tied her wrists together and left her lying near the rocky verge while he went after the Lazy S horse.

He caught up the gelding's trailing reins and led the animal back, tying it near the unconscious girl. Then he trotted to the rocks and brush and led his own mount out and back on to the trail.

He stood a moment, listening, but no sounds of pursuit came across the warm, gentle breeze. He caught up the money sack and secured it to the saddle of his own mount. The whole business had taken less than five minutes, yet it would not be long before Etta began to stir.

He knelt down and removed the brilliant bandanna from her face and neck, substituting his own dark blue one and adjusting it loosely around her neck.

Despite the seriousness of it all, Dave's mouth widened to a grin as he tied Etta's neckpiece around his own bronzed throat. He could not help wondering what she would think; whether she would recognize the dark blue kerchief, whether in fact she would guess who her unknown attacker had been.

He saw that a bruise was already forming on her chin where he had hit her, but she was breathing evenly and deeply and he loosened the rawhide on her wrists so that she would be able to free her hands within a short space of time.

He regarded her expensive rig-out and muttered: *Me an' Etta, too; we's both fools, I reckon!*

He leaned forward, kissing her softly on the mouth and marvelling at the beauty of her with her face so utterly in repose. Then he straightened up and went into the saddle, casting one last quick look around before he gently rowelled his mount and sent it speeding towards Signal on a wide, circling course.

No doubt he would have some heavy explaining to do when it came to telling Signal's bank and the marshal how he had found the money sack lying discarded on the road north out of town. But the thought was not serious enough to wipe the grin from Dave's dust-caked lips as he galloped towards his immediate destination ...

Slowly Etta's eyes opened and she found herself staring up into the blinding sun.

The moment she attempted to move, she discovered that her wrists were tied, and recollection flooded into her and with it she felt an impotent rage that left her shaking and half-crying.

She had achieved what she believed to be a brilliant, single-handed hold-up, only to be robbed of her spoils by some unknown high-grader at the moment when success had seemed certain!

With a kind of vicious concentration she applied herself to the task of freeing her hands and was surprised when the rawhide thongs came away without much trouble.

She sat there in the yellow dust, nursing her hurts both mental and physical. She gazed at her horse for several minutes and suddenly realized that it had been left securely tied for her!

Something else occurred to Etta Storm as she got up and began brushing the mica-particled dust from her clothes. Her wrists had not been properly tied! *Whoever had done this thing to her could not have intended her any harm!*

She began casting around for sign and eventually discovered tracks leading from a pile of boulders beside the trail. She searched around for a while, just to make certain sure that the money sack *had* been taken. She could guess now most of what had happened. Someone had lain in wait for her behind those rocks; had roped her and jerked her from the saddle. Gently she fingered the lump on her chin, wondering whether it had come by accident or design.

Well, the less Frank and the boys knew about this, the better, Etta told herself bitterly. She had been thoroughly outsmarted by someone. Someone who must have planned this little trick with care and ability.

She thought of Lonny, with his suspicious and meaningful glances, and wondered whether this could be some of his work. But she shook her head. What would be the point of it all? Besides which, even Lonny would scarcely dare to pull a stunt like this, with Frank to reckon with later on.

Nor had the mysterious ambusher taken her guns, or anything else that she could see. Just the money!

It was no Johnny Lawman, that was for sure, else he would have hauled her back to Signal.

Mystified and still somewhat shaken, Etta untied the reins and stepped into the saddle and began heading back along the road.

She felt cheated, as though someone were playing her along and taking a cruel delight in exposing her weaknesses; her inability to match either her physical strength or her wits with the opposite sex.

She thought of Cass Weidman and quickly shook her head. Even if, by some remote chance, Cass had come along at the right time, he would never have had the brains or strength—*Strength!* The word seemed almost like a key, opening a lock which hitherto had defied all attempts to spring it.

She reined in for a moment, sitting quite still and thinking of the way Dave

Starr had caught her up the other evening and had carried her silently and with consummate ease from the ranch house.

Dave Starr! Why had she not thought of him before? Yet Dave had said—well, he had told her things in the moonlight and had looked at her in such a way and had even asked her to marry him, just so he could 'save' her! But if Dave *had* robbed her, then it meant he was no better than Frank or any of the boys. Just another mealy-mouthed bastard! she thought, and wiped the sweat from her face and found herself looking at the dark blue neckpiece and remembering his steady gaze that day in the livery and his dark-shadowed face the night he had stood so close to her and had kissed her when the moonlight was touching the grass with its silvery light.

Savagely she wiped the wetness from her eyes and urged her mount forward and southward towards the Lazy S.

Though the town of Signal itself was not visible beyond the undulating grassland, Dave could see the mesa top from where he had watched things a while back. He judged that he was about two miles to the east of Signal, but to make it look right he still had to come in from the north or north-east.

He raised up in the saddle and saw no sign of riders as yet. He climbed down and tied his mount securely and hefted the sack of money over to a shallow, dry wash. Then he placed it carefully on the ground, stood back about fifteen paces and took careful aim.

As he had intended, the slug scorched its way through the top of the sack, just below the rawhide which Etta had used to fasten it. He replaced the gun in its holster without ejecting the spent load, humped the sack back to his horse and re-tied it to the saddle.

Then he mounted up and headed north at a fast lick and gradually began circling round until he found a wagon trail north of town.

He had barely hit the trail when a group of riders burst into view atop a rise about a half-mile distant.

Dave reined in and lifted his arm and watched the armed posse as it raced towards him.

There were nine men in all and the leader wore a star on his shirt, and Dave judged that this would be Marshal Wilcox.

They looked like farmers for the most part, but each carried a pistol or rifle and their sun-burned, bearded faces reflected at this moment little beyond a hard-eyed hostility.

They drew up in a cloud of dust not more than twenty yards from where Dave waited and the marshal's pistol was pointed straight at Dave.

'You know why we's here, Mister?' he demanded, and showed a faint surprise as Dave nodded and said: 'I reckon you must've had a robbery some while back and now you're fixin' to get the bandit and recover the *dinero?*' Dave shook his head. 'I doubt that you'll catch up with the robber—'

'See here!' one of the men shouted, brandishing a shot-gun. 'What kinda double-talk you givin' us, Mister? Ain't that our money you got right there in that wheat sack?'

The grey-haired marshal turned a suspicious eye on Dave. 'How come you know anything about a robbery?'

Dave sighed audibly so that these farmers could judge just how patient a man he was.

'My name's Dave Starr and a while back I was ridin' along plumb peaceable when all of a sudden a rider comes racin' along like a bat outa hell!'

'Go on,' Wilcox said grimly.

'Sure looked to me,' Dave said, 'that this fella was up to no good, what with the way he was fannin' the breeze an' this bulging wheat sack across his saddle!'

'Did you say *fella*, Mr Starr?'

Again Dave nodded. 'Sure. What else?'

'For your information,' Wilcox said coldly, 'the bank in Signal was robbed just over an hour back *and the bandit was a woman!*'

Dave Starr shrugged. 'Mebbe it was. I didn't get that close. I reckon I just figgered it was a man—'

'All right,' Wilcox snapped. 'So you saw a rider comin' from town and carryin' a bulging wheat sack! What did you do, and why was you suspicious, if that's what you say?'

'A man don't ride like that less'n it's a matter of life or death. I knew there was a town ahead, so I figgered the rider was runnin' away. When I saw this wheat sack, it seemed likely to me that the fella was a thief. Mebbe he even stole the horse.

'Anyways, I called out but he wouldn't—'

'We just done told you it was a woman!' Wilcox snapped.

'Oh, sure. Reckon I ain't ever heard of a woman bandit, but I wasn't close enough to argue the point with you.'

'What happened next?'

Dave smiled. 'I tried a shot just to scare the rider, but my slug musta gone clean through the sack. Look! You can see—' Dave held the sack clear of the saddle and Wilcox kneed his horse forward, taking care not to place himself between Starr and the posse men.

In a moment Wilcox looked up, glancing

across to the men. 'There sure is a bullet hole like he says. Mebbe he's tellin' the truth at that.' He turned back to Dave. 'You had a look in that sack, Mr Starr?'

'Why, sure. The rider, man or woman— whatever you say—didn't waste time comin' back for the sack. It was sure some fluke shot of mine!' Dave laughed, but no-one else seemed to think the thing was funny.

'What then?'

'Well, like I said, I opened the sack an' I cain't say I was surprised to see it packed with *dinero*. It's what I'd figgered all along.'

'Pretty smart, Mr Starr. Mind if I have your gun a minute?'

Dave handed his gun across, butt first, and watched the marshal sniff the barrel and examine the loads.

'One empty load an' the gun just bin fired like you claim.' He handed the weapon back and took the sack from Dave's unresisting grasp. He said: 'If what you say is true, you won't mind ridin' back with us to town?'

Dave shrugged in resignation. 'Just so it doesn't take too long ...'

It was starlight time and the moon was climbing when Dave finally found his way back to the cabin.

'What in tarnation you bin up to, Dave?' an anxious Ridout demanded.

The other grinned in the light of the two hurricane lamps. 'I'm plumb wore down with starvation, George. How about some o' that bacon an' beans you got cookin'?'

Ridout grunted and ladled a vast mess of hot victuals on to a tin plate. He sat Injun fashion on the floor, waiting with a full patience until Dave was through eating.

Then the scout got up and poured coffee into two tin mugs. He said: 'What about your hunch, Dave?'

'Yeah. I was right. In fact I practically watched her hold up the bank at Signal an' get clean away!'

'That ain't all!'

Dave grinned. 'Not by a jug-full, as you well know. I roped her, George, and

236

blindfolded her an' returned the *dinero* to Signal's bank—'

'How come they weren't suspicious of you?'

'They were. But by the time they'd heard my story, the town marshal was beginning to believe me. After that, I agreed to go back with them. Well, soon as the bank teller saw me, I was in the clear. He swore he had bin held up by a masked girl. He said I was at least a foot taller than the bandit who'd held a gun on him.'

'So they let you go! An' Etta?'

'Reckon she's back at the Lazy S, feelin' pretty sore in more ways than one!'

'How long you figger you can go on coverin' up for the kitten, Dave? How long before it's *her* gun as kills someone; or worse, how long before Carter does somethin' like callin' in the army, mebbe?'

'You think he'd do that?'

'Wal, I guess not. Not unless the Sutter gang gets really outa hand an' starts in raidin' all over Carter's territory.'

'Yeah. I know it cain't go on indefinitely,

George. It's just that I need some breathin' time. Mebbe we'll haveta try that idea of baitin' a trap for the Sutter boys.'

'As to that,' Ridout said, his eyes gleaming in the lamplight, 'the army payroll will be comin' into Fort Bliss at the end of the month. Mebbe we could flush them niggers from cover with a real temptin' bait, huh?'

Dave stared. 'You mean—?'

'Cap'n Boone might agree to sech a trick, 'specially if he knew who you was workin' for an' that you saved half of our Company at Antietam Creek. Y'see Dave, Cap'n Boone lost his two brothers there. I guess mebbe he'd like to meet you, anyways.'

'But we cain't have soldiers involved in this,' Dave objected. 'I don't see—'

Ridout shook his head. 'Won't be, way I got it figgered; only the wagon driver, mebbe. You an' me, Dave, we rig ourselves out in uniforms an' ride along with the pay wagon as a trooper escort.'

'By God, George! It might work at that. Only trouble is, can the two of us tackle the whole gang an' still look out for Etta?'

'Mebbe she won't ride this time. If she does, then it'll be up to you, Dave. Me, I ain't worried over takin' on seven-eight bushwhackers. I had my time, Dave, an' I ain't got any regrets; well, not many.'

But long before Ridout's plan could ever be put into operation, Etta was to strike again and earn for herself a killer's reputation ...

CHAPTER THIRTEEN

Bandit Queen

Marshal Elliot Wilcox sat in the sheriff's office in Mesquite. Across from him were Carter himself and deputy Jake Sepple.

'What's the trouble, Marshal?' Carter asked. 'Don't often see you here in Mesquite.'

Wilcox wiped dust and sweat from his

seamed face and Sepple arose and poured hot coffee into tin mugs and handed them round. Wilcox drank his down in one grateful gulp, wiped his greying moustache.

'That's a fact, but I heard *you* bin' havin' trouble, Sheriff; a bank hold-up and a stage robbery. I came over to see if we might compare notes because, two days back Signal's bank was held up an' robbed an' we got a detailed description of the bandit.'

'*You what?*' Carter exploded.

Wilcox grinned. He could afford to enjoy this moment. He was only a small town marshal and Carter was sheriff of the entire county. Yet it was obvious that, thanks to Dalston at the bank, Signal was one up on Mesquite.

Wilcox nodded. 'That's right. An' I figgered your robberies and ours might be the work of the same person.'

'Wal, I dunno. You say you've got a description of *the* bandit, meaning one man, whereas we know the bank job was done by four men and the stage was the work of eight or so desperadoes.'

'Mebbe,' Jake Sepple suggested, 'Signal's bank was held up by one of the same gang, Sheriff, goin' it alone?'

'It's possible,' Carter acknowledged thoughtfully. He turned to Wilcox. 'Even so, we'd sure appreciate that description.'

The town marshal nodded and grinned. 'It was a girl, Sheriff, about five feet six inches tall and weighing somewhere around one hun'ed and twen'y six pounds. She was dressed in fancy duds; a fringed ridin' skirt, bright coloured vest, red bandanna an' dun-coloured hat! How's that for a description?'

'A *girl*, you say?' Carter's face showed both disappointment and surprise. He shook his head. 'Sounds crazy, and it sure doesn't tie in with what *we* got.'

'Which is—?'

'We figured four men were involved in the bank robbery here at Mesquite. Leastways, we found tracks of four horses. Unfortunately, both bank employees on duty at that time were shot dead an' no-one else seems to have noticed anything.'

'And the Express stage?'

'We had a witness to that,' Carter replied, 'but there wasn't any mention of a girl. Just seven-eight masked men seen robbing the stage by a fella who was ridin' along about a mile back.'

Marshal Wilcox frowned and then something seemed to click in his brain. 'That's funny, you tellin' about a fella amblin' along an' seein' the hull thing!'

'What's so funny?'

'Just that when me an' the posse rode out after this girl, we run smack into some jasper who claimed he'd shot at the bandit an' missed. But he didn't miss the sack of stolen money. He was totin' it along, cool as all get-out!'

'What did he look like?' Sepple asked quickly.

Wilcox shrugged. 'Tough lookin' hombre; tall with black hair, clean-shaven, usual range clothes an' wearin' a .36 Navy Colt's gun.'

Carter's gaze pinned itself to his deputy's face. 'Jake,' he said, 'there sure is somethin' funny goin' on around here, like Mr Wilcox says. Wouldn't you say this description fits Dave Starr?'

'Like a glove, Sheriff,' Sepple grunted. 'Mebbe this girl an' Starr is workin' together?'

'There's one thing I forgot to tell you,' Wilcox cut in. 'An' I reckon it's purty dam' unusual. It's about the girl. The bank teller got a good look at her, that's how we got the description, but he also said she had deep black hair an' she was wearin' it loose around her shoulders!'

Carter shook his head. 'It's sure a detailed description and I'll get notices out on the strength of it; but it don't fit anyone I can think of. What about you, Jake?'

Sepple, too, shook his head. 'You'd think a woman wearin' a rig-out like that'd be known all over the territory.'

'Mebbe she would, Jake, unless she's only just started in on this line of work! But what about Dave Starr? He said he was goin' to Brownfield, didn't he?'

Jake nodded. 'Even if we picked him up, I doubt whether we'd get a durn thing outa

243

him. Like Mr Wilcox said, he's a tough hombre all right.'

Carter rose from his desk and began pacing the room, a cigar between his clenched teeth. He didn't want to tell Wilcox that he was certain that the Missouri bravos were responsible for all these crimes. The old fool might figure on trying to capture them with a farmers' posse. He might even have some success and reap all the glory and profit for himself. No! The less anyone knew about Frank Sutter's gang, the better for Sheriff Jack Carter.

As for this woman bandit; well, witnesses had made such mistakes before, either because they were fools or for some motives of fear or gain.

It might well be that Sutter had a girl rider in his gang. It had happened before; what about Belle Starr?

At this moment a horse pulled up outside in a flurry of dust and noise, and footsteps echoed across the boardwalk. The three lawmen looked up as Deputy Herb Rayner burst into the room.

His face and clothes were white with dust except where the sweat had made darker runnels on his face. He was panting a little and his eyes were bright with the excitement of his news.

'Sheriff!'

'What is it, Herb?'

'Just got the news from Brownfield! A farmer name o' Buck Weidman's bin shot dead by a young girl in fringed ridin' skirt and black an' gold bolero!'

'Who says?'

'Cass Weidman, the old man's boy. Said he saw everythin' but the girl held a gun on him an' escaped!'

'Where is this Cass Weidman?'

'He's over to Brownfield, tellin' his story left an' right. I told him not to leave the farm 'case you might wanta question him.'

'The Bandit Queen, Sheriff!' Wilcox said. 'What I tell you? You was for disbelievin' what I said about a girl, wasn't you?'

'I—I dunno. I ain't sure. Looks like you an' your bank teller was right, anyway. I'll haveta ride over an' see this Weidman boy. The hell of it is, Brownfield's strong for the South an' the marshal there rode with the Confederates!'

'You want I should get a posse together?' Sepple asked.

'No. That'd tip our hand. We gotta play this carefully. This girl isn't on her own, of that I'm sure ...'

On the way back to the Lazy S, Etta had ample time to think about what she had done and what she had failed to do.

Quite objectively and without conceit, she knew that the robbery itself, without any detailed planning, had been an inspiration. But where she had failed so abysmally was in allowing herself to be roped, knocked unconscious and robbed of the money she had so successfully taken.

She was sure now that it had been Dave Starr. No-one else could fit the rôle, and that was one other hombre to get even with one fine day.

Meanwhile there was this question of Frank and the boys. At first she had figured to say nothing. But as she rode along the thought became borne home to her that likely Frank or Lonny or maybe Doc would somehow hear about it all. They might well learn that a young girl dressed exactly as she was dressed had held up and robbed Signal's bank. And, if Frank did discover that she was hiding things from him and acting without orders, he might well throw her to the wolves, if nothing else.

The day was beginning to fade as Etta off-saddled her mount and turned it into the pole corral. Jim Sutter was sitting on the porch steps and gave her a cheerful smile.

'You look dam' fine, Etta, but ain't those clothes a mite conspicuous?'

She smiled. Perhaps of all these hard-case young men, she liked Jim the best, though it would never do to let Frank know. 'Scared, Jim, that I'll be identified more easily as one of the Sutter gang?'

Jim grinned back, yet there was a faint scary look in back of his eyes. Something about Etta Storm bothered Jim Sutter at that moment, but he had no notion what it might be, and after a while he returned to his whittling.

'Frank,' Etta announced the moment she entered Sutter's room, 'I got somethin' to tell you!'

The big man looked up and his blue-eyed gaze ran over her face and figure with a warmth that caused her cheeks to flame.

'Hell-an'-be-merry, Etty! I ain't ever seen you lookin' so lovely. No. Not even that day when you was lyin' in the hay in Weidman's barn!'

'I told you I got somethin' important to say. When you hear it, mebbe you'll throw me out or shoot me or somethin'—'

Frank's eyes hardened. 'If it's as bad as that, kid, you better spit it out dam' quick.'

As it happened, Frank was alone for once and Etta sank down into the chair normally occupied by Doc Dufresne.

'Ain't any use beatin' around, I reckon,' she said. 'The truth is, Frank, I held up Signal's bank an' robbed it—'

'*You what?*'

She nodded, almost resigned now to the wrath to come. 'I figgered I did a good job, an' so I did—at first—'

'Wait a minute, Etty! You tellin' me you robbed Signal's bank *and* got away clear or have you got some goddam' posse trailin' you right now to this place?'

'No posse, Frank. No money, either, 'cos I lost that on the way, like a stupid fool!'

'Mebbe,' Frank said softly, 'you'd better tell it from the beginnin'.'

He listened in silence while she told exactly what had happened, not sparing herself when it came to the part where she had been knocked unconscious and robbed.

'You any idea who this hombre was?' Frank asked when she had finished.

She shook her head. 'Some high-grader who figgered there was money in the sack—'

'Someone who didn't want you to recognize him, seems likely to me—'

'Then why didn't he just wear a mask an'

hold me up?' Etta argued, and Frank shook his head and sat for a while, thinking.

'You figgered I was gonna be mad with you, didn't you? You told me all this because you knew that sooner or later I'd hear the bank had bin robbed by a masked girl?'

'What you goin' to do?'

He said: 'You did better'n I'd ever figured, Etta, 'specially the way you circled round to shake off any likely pursuers. I guess you was dam' unlucky to lose the *dinero* like you did, less'n, o' course, you stashed it away for yourself an' made up that part o' the story!'

She came over to the bed and stood gazing down at him, her cheeks aflame and her eyes dark and glittering.

'I swear it's true, every word of it. I could take you or any of the boys to the exact spot—'

'As it happens,' he said, 'I believe what you told me. Only thing I don't like is some unknown jasper hornin' in and the fact you done acted without orders.'

'I know. I—I guess I shouldn't have tried

it. It was just that it seemed so easy—the street almost empty—an' that two-bit bank just beggin' to be robbed!'

Frank grinned wolfishly but his blue eyes were less like chips of ice than they had been at the beginning.

'You should 'a' killed that bank employee, Etta, an' you could 'a' done so easy, even if he did move at your first shot. Now the marshal an' everyone in Signal will be on the look-out for a girl dressed like you, an' there sure ain't two of you, not in the whole country.'

She nodded. She wasn't going to tell Frank that she had had no stomach for an unnecessary killing. If it had been Cass or Weidman himself, she might have acted very differently.

She said now: 'These clothes, Frank. If everyone's goin' to be looking for me just on account of what I'm wearin' then the easiest thing is to get rid of them.'

'Not less'n you want to. Frank Sutter don't allow himself or his boys to be pushed around by anyone. That's why I ain't mad at you. True, we cover our faces on a raid, like you did, but that's all. We don't bother changin' our names or anythin' like that. You was here at the ranch all day, if it comes to that, an' I got six-seven witnesses as can swear to it. No, I ain't worried about the law. It ain't worth a plugged dollar.'

Etta said: 'I'd sure like to ride over an' see Weidman an' make him eat dirt.'

'After what he did to you, I cain't say as I blame you. Whyn't you go and see him tomorrow an' make him crawl on his belly?'

She smiled wickedly and leaned forward and kissed him. 'It'll give me the greatest pleasure ...'

As soon as everyone was through eating breakfast, Etta cleared away with the help of Jesse Lindquist and Jim. All of Sutter's gang knew about Weidman and the bad time he had given Etta, and both Jesse and Jim nodded their approval when she told them where she was going.

Jim went out and saddled a horse, and shortly Etta came out of the ranch wearing her new clothes and looking as though she had stepped from the pages of a picture book. She patted Jim's arm and took the reins and swung into the saddle, heading towards Weidman's place.

She could not help experiencing a feeling of triumph that Frank had taken her story the way he had. Not that she had lied or even concealed the truth; only in one respect at least, and that was with regard to the identity of her attacker. Was she trying to shield Dave? she wondered. If so, she was a fool, for the man was the worst kind of thief; a high-grader who let others do the dirty work and then robbed them when the way was clear.

She shook her head in uncertainty, searching for evil motives where none existed and even applying this cruel probing to her own actions. She tried hard and almost successfully to convince herself that she would just as lief kill a man as look at him.

But the wind whipped the colour into her lips and cheeks and drove away these darker thoughts, and for the first time she grew aware of the beauty around her; the sun drawing the dew from the sage brush and the breeze rippling the grass and turning it into a surging yellow sea.

But the moment she crested the ridge and gazed down on to those hateful buildings which themselves seemed saturated with Weidman's loathsome character, her whole mood changed.

She rode on down the slope, her face hard and her lips crooked into a smile utterly devoid of humour.

A fire was sending up a spiral of smoke near to the stable and the clink of hammer on metal told her that either Buck or Cass was likely shoeing one of the draught horses.

It was Cass, for at that moment Weidman emerged from the house, shading his eyes and gazing at this magnificently garbed creature with a kind of shocked incredulity.

Etta came on and reined in the gelding less than a dozen paces from Buck. She pushed back her hat, allowing him a good look at her face and the hatred and contempt that lay there unmasked.

'*Etta!*' It was all Weidman seemed capable of saying at the moment as he stood stock still with gaze riveted upon this changed girl.

She got down and looped a rein over the rack by the house.

'Is that all you got to say?' she sneered. 'Ain't you goin' to ask me what I'm doin' here, or—'

It was then that Weidman surprised her, more than he had ever done before. He was like an evil lizard; one moment as still as a stone and the next, darting forward with arms outstretched and clawlike hands grabbing at her neck.

The very force of his thrust as well as the shocking unexpectedness of it sent Etta crashing to the ground with Weidman on top of her. She could not reach for either gun; her hands were around Weidman's wrists as she struggled in a desperate sweat of fear to ease that remorseless pressure around her neck. She felt herself choking, and the hateful face so close to hers began to swim out of focus, as in a nightmare dream.

From some way off she heard what sounded like the quick drum of boots, but she could not be sure. Then, with a supreme effort, she managed to shift Weidman slightly to one side and at the same time she brought a knee up into the pit of his stomach.

The stranglehold on her neck eased and she felt herself gasping for air, wondering dimly whether these brief moments would buy her the time and strength she needed.

Again the sound of footsteps came, this time nearer and louder, and a rifle barked out and she felt Weidman's body arch and jerk and he was falling away from her, his face ghastly in its pallor and his eyes rolling until they became fixed in death.

She looked up into the grinning face of Cass. He was holding a smoking .22 and the expression on his face told Etta that he was as crazy as Buck whom he had so cold-bloodedly killed.

'I saved you from him, Etty! He'd 'a' choked you to death ef'n it hadn't bin for me!' He lowered the rifle, shot a quick glance at the lifeless body and brought his gaze back to Etta just in time to see death staring him in the face!

She was still on the ground but she had twisted over on to her side and reached for her right-hand gun in one and the same movement. What Cass Weidman saw was not only the gaping hole of a Colt's muzzle, but murder in those dark blue velvety eyes of Etta Storm's.

The whole action had taken the girl no more than a few seconds, despite her distraught condition and the bruises around her throat, and now the gun's hammer was back and her forefinger tightened on the trigger, sending the slug screaming into the breech of Cass Weidman's rifle and smashing the weapon from his hand.

Slowly she got up, facing him all the while and knowing that he was crazy to have her; knowing, too, that he was scarcely aware of what he had done.

'Touch me, Cass, or come a step closer an' I'll blast you to the gates of hell!'

She heard the words as though someone

other than herself had spoken them. But they had their marked effect on Cass and he stood rooted to the spot, scarce moving a muscle as she untied her mount and went into the saddle. He was still standing there, his right arm numb, the smashed rifle at his feet, when she disappeared from view over the ridge. Then he turned and made for the barn and saddled up, talking to himself all the while and saying: 'If I cain't have her, then nobody else will ...'

CHAPTER FOURTEEN

Trap for Bushwhackers

When Starr shook hands with Captain Boone, commander at Fort Bliss, both men realized that this was not the first time they had met.

Boone had been in command of a Company that had fought right alongside Dave's Troop.

'The 6th Illinois, wasn't it, Mr Starr, and this side-winder Ridout was scouting for the whole shebang?'

Dave smiled. 'That's right, Cap'n. There's many names I forgotten from Antietam Creek, but not faces.'

Boone nodded and waved Dave and the scout to a couple of chairs in the barely furnished office.

'I can still remember something of what you did there, Mr Starr, and now Ridout's told me a little of what's been going on around here and also who you are working for. If there's anything I can do, give me the word, 'specially if it's going to help nail the hides of those Sutter killers!'

'Thanks, Cap'n. That's exactly what we's aimin' to do. But first off, how is Henry Forrest? It is true that you got him right here in the fort?'

Boone nodded. 'Sure, and thanks to a strong constitution and Dr Kroeg's efforts, it looks like Forrest will not only live, but recover sufficiently to give his evidence.

'We heard most of the story from Doc McCready and Jake Sepple. You did a good job, Mr Starr, in bringing back the coach and its human freight!'

Dave showed a meagre smile. 'But I didn't bring back the pay-roll. Tell me, Cap'n, did Forrest still have the slug in him when he was brought here?'

Captain Boone showed mild surprise. 'Why, no. Doc McCready got it out and tended Forrest first, before handing him over to us. Why do you ask?'

'Was just wonderin' whether it was a rifle or pistol slug.'

Boone frowned. 'Guess I don't rightly remember, but McCready could tell—wait a minute! I *do* remember now. The doc said he figured it had come from a .36 calibre pistol.'

'And what about Ed Coles?'

'You mean the other special messenger; the one who was killed in the coach? That I don't know about, Mr Starr. Again it was McCready who examined him.'

Dave nodded. He said: 'Me an' Ridout's got a tough chore ahead of us, Cap'n Boone, an' we'll need all the help we can get.

'To cut it short, we's fixin' to flush the Sutter boys an' their gang out into the open. The bait I was hopin' to use, with your permission an' help, is the paymaster's wagon at the end of this month.'

Boone smiled grimly. 'I guess mebbe if I stuck to the book of rules, I'd have to say "No". But I've already said I'll help if it's at all feasible.'

Dave rolled a cigarette and fired it. He said: 'George has already told me the pay-roll allus comes along the stage road from Cottonwood Junction at the end of the month.

'My plan is simply to spread the news around so's Sutter and his boys'll hear of it; let them know that mebbe twen'y thousand dollars'll be on that road and with only a small escort.'

'They'd have to be volunteers, Mr Starr.'

'Sure; but George an' me'll make two, provided the army will loan us uniforms for this once. All we want then is a volunteer driver an' a sharpshooter ridin' up beside him.'

'You think just four men can tackle the Sutter bunch?'

Ridout spoke for the first time: 'Look, Cap'n; they ain't ordinary God-fearin' Johnny Rebs, you know that. They's yeller-bellied bushwhackers an' I'd give anythin' to git a crack at them.'

'There's just one thing that occurs to me,' Captain Boone said. 'Why don't you tell the sheriff in Mesquite you're a Pinkerton man; enlist his help and organize a posse of men who can ride and shoot?'

Dave had some explaining to do and he knew it. He told, then, about Etta Storm; everything he knew. At the worst she was a thief driven to this life by the harsh treatment meted out by her own kinsfolk.

'There's somethin' else, too,' he said, when he had finished the story. 'Somehow or other I don't quite trust Carter. Oh, I know he's a Federal man and I reckon a good peace officer, but even now I'm scared he might go off half-cocked an' try ambushin' the Sutters at their ranch.'

Boone nodded. 'Likely you're right, and

that would mean the girl being in grave danger, perhaps being killed for crimes which, as far as you know, she has not committed.'

Boone went over to his desk, picked up a quill pen and pulled an officially stamped sheet of paper towards him.

'You, Ridout, will have to ride into Cottonwood Junction beforehand and give this note personally to Major Dringle, the pay-master.'

'Sure. The major knows me, anyways.'

Dave said: 'As I understand it from George here, the money is hauled to Cottonwood Junction by special coach on the 27th of each month. That means we'll both need to be there on the day preceding. We'll arrange with Major Dringle to have the money bags filled with stones and such like, just in case anyone's watching when the pay-wagon is loaded up.'

Boon signed his name with a flourish. 'A good idea, Mr Starr. In fact, the more I think of this little scheme the more I like it, though God knows what Washington would say if they knew.' He clasped his hands together and regarded Dave steadily. 'You may already know that I lost my two brothers at the bloody fighting at Antietam Creek. Yet, after all, that was war. What you may not know is, that it was some of Maury's men, including the Sutters, who raided behind the lines and burned my farm to the ground and killed my parents.'

Dave said quietly: 'I didn't know, Cap'n, but you can rest assured we'll do our best to get these bushwhackers. They make a stench in the nostrils of any honest Johnny Reb!'

Ridout said: 'As to the men, sir, I'd like Sergeant Flynn an' Trooper Stredder if they's willin'.'

'I guess they'll be ready to volunteer,' Boone smiled. 'I'll send for them right away. But first, there's one other thing.' He turned to Dave. 'How do you propose to circulate this story of a heavy pay-roll, so it will reach the ears of Sutter and his men?'

Dave frowned. 'I bin thinkin' about that, Cap'n, and it's not gonna be too easy, with only me an' George—'

Boone nodded. 'I think I can help you there; my idea is to send a re-mount officer and two troopers into Brownfield, ostensibly to purchase new horses. They will, of course, be told beforehand of their real mission. I think you may rely on them to get sufficiently 'drunk' to shoot off their mouths and circulate the story for the ears of Sutter and his men.'

'That'd sure be a great help, Cap'n.'

Boone rose from his desk, opened the door and called his orderly. 'Find Sergeant Flynn and Trooper Stredder and bring them here at the double, Bates.'

Shortly, there was a knock at the door and Flynn and Stredder entered, standing stiffly to attention until the captain ordered them at ease.

Flynn grinned all over his rugged face at sight of Ridout and his companion. The sergeant could smell a little action here and he didn't much care what it was. Stredder, too, was a tough, rawboned man who had fought Indians as well as Southerners, and his dark eyes flickered with interest as Captain Boone swore them to secrecy and outlined the plan.

'You understand, both of you,' he said, 'that this is not an order. Mr Ridout and Mr Starr have asked for volunteers. It is a dangerous game that we are playing and does not come within the normal line of duty. If you were detailed to guard an actual pay-roll, that would be a different thing. But what in fact you will be doing is to defend a decoy wagon containing nothing of value whatsoever!'

Flynn shot Stredder a quick sideways glance and his bearded face broke into a smile of sheer delight. 'When do we start, Cap'n? ...'

On the face of it, the plan by which Dave hoped to break the power of the Sutter gang, seemed simple enough. Yet, when they got down to cases, both Dave and Ridout found that there were many details to be hammered out; many snags which might well wreck the whole scheme.

With Sergeant Flynn and Trooper Stredder they studied the map of the stage road from Cottonwood Junction to Mesquite and Fort Bliss.

Ridout saw the quartermaster about uniforms and Dave briefed the men who were going to ride to Brownfield within the next two days.

It was dusk by the time the major issues had been settled, yet there still remained a few more details to discuss and Captain Boone suggested that the two men stayed at the post overnight ...

In the morning, Boone sent for Dave Starr and waved him to a chair.

'I've been thinking about Sheriff Carter, Mr Starr, and I reckon you're right to be concerned about him.'

'You figger he'll mebbe make a raid an' spoil our plan?'

Boone smoothed his iron-grey moustache before replying. He said: 'I've met Carter several times and, like you said, he's a good enough lawman except mebbe he's got a little bounty-hunter blood in his veins. I've got an idea how we might keep Carter busy the next few days.'

Dave grinned. He had taken quite a

shine to this rather stern-faced army veteran who, since the war, had found himself commanding a post in the wilderness. 'Tell me, Cap'n,' Dave said.

'There's a patrol due in today from Lone Jack. They rode out a week ago to keep an eye on a small band of Comanches.' Boone leaned forward and there was a gleam in his eyes as he went on. 'They *could* be reporting a little trouble such as horse-stealing; mebbe even a suspected killing. If such is the case and it is purely a civil matter, I would, of course, hand it over to the sheriff, who would be bound to ride out and investigate. You see?'

'Sure.' Dave grinned. 'But isn't it likely he'll come back on you, Cap'n?'

Boone shrugged. 'Mebbe my patrol was jumpy or mebbe the trouble was cleared up before Sheriff Carter got there. *Quien sabe,* as they say in this God-forsaken State!'

By the afternoon, Lieutenant Scott and two troopers were on their way to Brownfield for the purchase of re-mounts and Dave and Ridout drifted quietly and without ceremony into Mesquite.

Dave's first port of call was at the telegraph office, and here he found a telegram awaiting him from Allan Pinkerton. It was an innocuous message in code and the operator handed it over with bored disinterest.

Outside on the boardwalk, Dave decoded the message. There was nothing here to cause him any change of plan. He was not to take fool risks and, if necessary, at least two more operatives could be sent if Dave judged it necessary.

Starr smiled as he crumpled the paper into a ball and threw it away. Pinkerton still had sufficient confidence in him to go on giving him *carte-blanche* and Dave fervently hoped that he would not let 'Major Allan' down.

He began moving down street to where he had left Ridout with the horses, but a rider burst on to Main and threw himself from the saddle in a cloud of dust and took the boardwalk outside the sheriff's office in three long strides.

Something was up and Dave had to know what it was. But, of a sudden, he saw Ridout way up there ahead. The scout was standing still and Dave knew that if anyone could find out what was going on, then Ridout could.

Some kind of hunch, or maybe sheer instinct, warned Dave to keep out of Carter's way this afternoon. He stood in a patch of shade and waited.

Ten minutes later, George came along the street leading both horses. He tied them to a rail and led Dave into the quiet of an adjoining alley.

'What's up, George? Was that one of Carter's deputies ridin' in hell for leather?'

Ridout nodded soberly. 'Bad news, Dave. I ketched dam' near everythin' he said. Etta's done gone an' killed Weidman, it seems. Leastways, the boy Cass is swearin' it's so, down in Brownfield!'

For a long moment Dave Starr stood utterly still. The sweat ran cold on his face and neck and a sick despair lay in his belly, and George Ridout did not like the look in his friend's eyes.

'Lookit, Davey! There's allus a chance et ain't so. Supposin' Rayner got it wrong

270

or—or supposin' even Cass was lyin'?'

Dave spun round and caught Ridout's arm in a grip that made the oldster wince. 'Mebbe you got somethin' there, George. Mebbe Cass *is* lyin' to save his own dirty rotten hide—'

'There's one way o' findin' out. You git to Brownfield fast. If the kid ain't there, he'll be back at the farm. I'll hold Carter, if I can, by tellin' him what Cap'n Boone said an' that there's a message due from the fort—'

Dave strode to the hitch rail and untied his mount. His uniform was wrapped in a gunny sack and this he handed over to Ridout.

'I'll meet you at the cabin tonight, George,' he said, and went into the saddle and sent his mount fairly flying from town.

The steel-dust responded gamely to its rider's harsh treatment and normally Dave Starr would never use a horse like this. For George might not be successful in delaying the sheriff and Dave had to get to Cass Weidman first. Somehow or other

271

he *had* to discover where the truth lay and the thought that even now Etta might be innocent of Weidman's killing was like a distant light of hope.

Twice only did Dave pull up his lathered mount for brief rests and then he was in Brownfield, having ridden some fifteen miles or so in a fraction over thirty-five minutes.

Half the town was buzzing with the news and it was not difficult for Dave to obtain his information and at the same time keep clear of Shiro Calvin. Cass Weidman had ridden in earlier, had gotten half drunk and spilled his sensational story to all who would listen.

The information that Herb Rayner had brought to the sheriff in Mesquite had been right enough. Cass claimed that Etta Storm had ridden down on the farm and had deliberately murdered his father in cold blood. What was even worse, she had shot him in the back. She had tried to kill Cass, too, but had only succeeded in knocking the rifle from his hands.

The brave Cass Weidman had then

gone after her and, frightened, the girl had fled.

Dave listened to the scraps of information and wondered grimly whether Shiro Calvin had yet ridden out to Weidman's place. He doubted it, but the whole business might well make Calvin's position delicate and embarrassing. This town, and the marshal with it, were so obviously pro-South. The Sutter boys were Southerners and that meant they were likely operating with Calvin's knowledge if not his actual backing. Yet a member of this community had been murdered by a girl who rode with Sutter. Maybe Brownfield didn't even know this fact yet, for it seemed that Cass Weidman had not mentioned the Sutters or any gang. Cass's main theme was that Etta was a wanton killer and ought to be strung up quick.

One thing was now out in the open, Dave realized as he rowelled the steel-dust along the dirt road; the identity of the mysterious girl bandit was no longer open to doubt. Cass had identified her as Etta Storm.

Dave found where to turn off, plunged across the waving grass and checked his mount at the top of the ridge. He saw the farm and its outbuildings and in a flash was tearing straight down the gentle slope at a dead gallop.

He had barely hit the hard-packed yard when a youngster came tumbling from the house, a rifle clenched in his hands. Dave came up closer, looking at the boy, knowing him to be Cass Weidman and disliking what he saw in that loose-lipped, mean-eyed face.

It was the boy's glance which dropped first, even as he began to bluster his way with a snarling question. 'Who are you, Mister, an' what you want?'

Dave slid from the saddle, walked close up to the boy so that Cass was forced to swing the rifle aside. Dave's quick eye saw then the bullet-smashed breech and knew that the rifle was useless as a lethal weapon. He also knew that in this part, at least, Cass Weidman's story had been true.

'What happened when Etta came back?

Tell me what happened.'

'How d'you know Etta came back an'—'

In a sudden fury Dave caught the boy, much as Weidman had held Etta. His hands closed around Cass's neck and he shook the youngster with a strength and ferocity that began to turn the boy's face a dark, reddish purple.

Dave let go then and, gasping for breath, Cass gagged out the story much as Dave had heard it in Brownfield.

'You buried your father yet?' Dave's voice was as cold as mountain ice.

'No. I dragged him over to the barn. I ain't had time—'

'Sure. You ain't had time, ridin' into Brownfield an' gettin' liquored up so's you could spill this crazy story!'

Weidman stared with unbelieving gaze. 'Crazy story? What you mean? It's the truth, I tell you, an' that harlot cousin o' mine's sure gonna hang or—'

Dave's fist shot out. There was a loud cracking noise as knuckles connected with jaw and Cass Weidman fell like a pole-axed steer.

Dave wiped the sweat from his eyes and for a moment murder shone through the glistening wetness of his face.

He began to move towards the barn which Cass had indicated but was swung sharply round by the rataplan of riding hooves. He saw that it was George Ridout and waited for the scout to come up.

Ridout said: 'Cap'n Lacey's jest arrived in Mesquite from the fort, Dave. Now Carter don't know whether to ride out here or what. Say, you tryin' to kill this runt?'

'Mebbe. Weidman's body's over to the barn.' Without waiting for an answer, Dave strode away while Ridout's gaze flickered over the scene. He looked for sign and found it some distance away. He was prepared to take a bet that the single tracks were the same as those he had found along near to the line cabin; in other words, he figured they were Etta's. He saw where the scuffle had taken place but elsewhere the sign was mussed up and almost impossible to read.

He tied his horse and went over to the

barn and found Dave looking down at the stiffening body of Buck Weidman.

George knelt down and managed to get the dead man out of his coat and vest. Then he turned him over on his belly.

He looked up at Dave. 'You get anythin' outa the kid?'

'Only what we already bin told. What you figger you're doin'?'

'Somethin' smells around here, Dave. There was a fight over to the yard right enough, but I ain't satisfied it happened like Cass Weidman says.'

'What you goin' to do?' Dave asked again.

Ridout took out his knife and inserted it into the wound in Weidman's back. He probed around for quite a while and Dave went outside and watched Cass Weidman show signs of returning consciousness.

A sharp yell from Ridout brought Dave back into the barn in double-quick time. The oldster held out his hand and there, nestling in the palm, was a small piece of blunted, blood-stained lead.

'That ain't from no .36 Navy Colt,

Dave! Did Etty have a rifle?'

Starr shook his head. 'No. Not even after she'd rigged herself out in Signal. She carried two guns but nary a rifle or carbeen. You mean—'

Ridout said tightly: 'My guess is that this slug's from that thar .22 rifle lyin' in the yard. What's more I'm beginnin' to get the picture. I don't reckon Etty shot Weidman at-all. I don't see how she could've. Buck Weidman was killed by his own son, Davey, or I'm the son of an Injun bitch!'

The sudden drumming of hooves came to the ears of both men and they moved quickly forward in time to see Cass Weidman board a saddler and sweeping out from behind the house.

'Do we bring the bastard down, Dave?'

'Let him go.'

All at once the sick despair had gone from Dave's stomach. He owed this swift change to the cunning of the old scout. But, more important by far than Dave's own feelings was the fact that, miraculously it seemed, Etta was still innocent. Oh, sure; mebbe she had tried to kill; mebbe even this time Cass had been right in saying she had ridden down on them with a gun in her hand. As for the other stage messenger inside the coach, Dave would have to check with McCleary whether he had been killed by a rifle or pistol slugs.

Dave took a deep breath. In a few days' time the final scene would be played if all went according to their plans. Was it still possible to save Etta Storm and at the same time nail the hides of Sutter and his gang ...?

CHAPTER FIFTEEN

Miracle in Santa Donna

Lonny dismounted in the yard, tied his horse and proceeded through the house to Frank's room.

The big man was restlessly pacing up and down and Lonny noticed that he had already discarded the black sling.

'You look like a caged bear, Frank,' he grinned. 'What—?'

'To hell with you an' your dam' jokes, Lonny! Much more o' bein' cooped up here an' I'll go ravin' mad. You oughta—'

'Hold it now, Frank, an' listen to what I got to say. Mebbe you ain't goin' to stay cooped up here much longer!'

'What you drivin' at?'

'Just this. I bin in Brownfield all day, an' what d'you think I found out from a coupla drunken soldiers?'

'You tell me!'

Lonny sat on the rumpled bed and built a cigarette. When he had finished, he stuck it in his mouth and looked up into his brother's face.

'Ain't like you to git all riled up, Frank, but mebbe this news'll cheer you some. There's an army pay-wagon comin' along the stage road from Cottonwood Junction on the 30th of this month. It'll be carryin' around twenty thousand bucks, mebbe more—'

'You figger we's strong enough to buck

the army?' Frank asked drily.

'You ain't heard it all yet,' the dark one said patiently. 'There's only goin' to be four-five troopers escortin' it at most!'

Frank stopped his pacing and considered the information in silence, his blue gaze now more calmly thoughtful.

'Sounds too good to be true,' he murmured at last. 'It ain't possible, surely? Why would they haul so much *dinero* and protect it with such a dam' measly escort?'

Lonny shook his head. 'You don't understand, Frank. Seems like they bin doin' this thing every month now and for so long it's become a habit. I tell you, those goddam Blue-bellies spilled a whole heap an' don't tell me they was playin' some game. They didn't know who I was—I doubt if they even saw me, they was so drunk!

'Then a loot'nant came in an' gave 'em a workin' over an' said they'd better git to hazin' those hosses dam' quick or he'd pussonally haul 'em up before the old man.'

Frank sat down, chewing his underlip. 'Sounds good, Lonny; sounds dam' good. If we could take a crack at them dam' Yankees an' line our pockets at the same time—'

'Why not? I tell you, it's a cinch, an' it's usually me who's the one to look for snags. Like Etty, f'r instance. I admit I figgered she might bring trouble at first; then, well, she did her part in everythin', leastways, right up until yesterday!'

'What you mean, Lonny? What's Etty gotta do with this thing? For God's sake spit it out!'

'Nothin' much, 'ceptin' that the Weidman boy was in town yesterday, claimin' that his cousin, Etta Storm, had done killed his paw—'

'*What?*'

'Sure. Seems like there was a lot of talk, then he moseyed back home to the farm. Etty came in late last evenin' but I ain't bin able to check on it yet on account I bin in Brownfield all of today.'

'By God! It's mebbe true at that. She told me she was gonna see Weidman an' make him crawl. Wal? Looks like she done it. What difference does it make?'

'Only that Cass Weidman has now positively identified the Bandit Girl as Etta Storm. That means the law can—'

'The law?' Frank sneered. 'What law? Do you figger Shiro Calvin's goin' to buck us? No! Not on your tin-type. Calvin won't do a durn thing about it, even if it is true!'

'What about the sheriff in Mesquite?'

Frank looked at his brother queerly. 'Since when was you scared of a tin star?'

Lonny flushed to the roots of his dark hair. 'You know me better'n that, Frank; I was just figgerin'—'

'Leave the figgerin' to me. First off, go find Etta. Likely she's with the hosses. After that, we're gonna have a meeting an' plan a nice little surprise for those goddam Blue-bellies!'

There had been a sharp thunderstorm overnight, but the rain had been short and sharp and had scarcely laid the dust.

The air was close and sticky, but as the sun climbed above the eastern hills it once more turned the land hot and dry.

The U.S. army wagon with its faded canvas top rumbled along the rutted road at the usual cavalry gait. Trooper Stredder, his face sweating but alert, drove the two-horse team. On the seat beside him, the bearded Sergeant Flynn squatted, grinning every so often as he surveyed the land ahead and on either side, through a service-battered pair of field glasses.

Two uniformed troopers trailed the slow-moving wagon, one on either side. It was astonishing what a difference the Federal uniforms made to the appearance of Ridout and Dave Starr. A man would have to ride mighty close to recognize either of them for what they were.

To all outward appearances, this was just another boring routine job; the pay-roll for Fort Bliss being hauled with an almost careless unconcern born of constant repetition. Yet both Dave and Ridout had Spencers in their saddle-boots and two more of the same ten-shot Carbeens lay at the feet of Flynn and Stredder; forty shots in all and without re-loading!

Everything had been planned with the careful precision of a full-scale military operation; but nothing was certain with regard to the Sutter gang and Dave and his men had only been able to guess at the likely points of ambush.

Yet they were not just blind guesses, but ones based upon a certain amount of hard-headed reasoning.

The Sutters would be coming from their ranch, yet they might well circle round and approach the road from a different direction. What was more certain was the fact that they would need some kind of cover both for the ambush itself—if it were attempted—and also to facilitate their getaway.

Ridout's eyes were almost as keen as Flynn's were with the glasses, and the scout's gaze was constantly on the stretches of thick underbrush and occasional formations of rock.

It was now well past the middle of the forenoon and the pay-wagon had left

Cottonwood Junction at seven o'clock. If nothing happened, they planned to pull into some shade before noon to rest and eat.

A half-mile or so up ahead, a line of cottonwoods cast a welcome shade across the arid road. Opposite were some rocks from which a few clumps of mesquite and piñon sprouted.

Ridout veered his mount alongside Dave's. He said, matter-of-factly: 'One o' the spots we picked out on the map, Davey.'

Starr's hand slid to the stock of his carbeen. This was perhaps one of the worst chores he had ever tackled.

'Tell Flynn,' he said in a dust-dry voice.

Ridout jerked his head, circled round the rear of the wagon and came up alongside Sergeant Flynn.

'See anythin', Sergeant?'

'Nary a thing; mebbe this hull thing's gonna fizzle out like a damp squib!'

'I dunno. I got a feelin',' Ridout said. 'Damned if I cain't smell sump'n—'

But before the scout had time to enlarge, a rifle barked out from behind the rocks and, as though this were a signal, others opened up until the air was thick with screaming lead.

As suddenly as the attack had come, Dave and his men reacted at once. In those first few minutes, when all hell seemed to have broken loose, Ridout and Dave had slid from their saddles, carbeens in hand. Flynn and Stredder were pouring lead from the driving seat, and there was no difficulty with a rearing team for both animals had been shot dead in their traces.

A yell went up from ahead, and on both sides of the road men began to appear, advancing steadily and firing as they came.

Though each outlaw was masked, Frank Sutter was easily recognizable, big and unafraid, standing in the middle of things, a smoking Colt in his right hand.

By now Stredder and Flynn had crawled from the seat back through the wagon and had dropped from the tail-gate to join Dave and Ridout who were crouched near the rear wheels.

For a moment or two, black powder smoke drifted across the scene, making things uncertain for both sides. Yet it gave Dave and the others time to re-load and when the smoke cleared they saw two of Sutter's men on the ground, either dead or wounded.

But for Frank and Lonny and the rest the situation was not quite so clear cut. They knew that two or three of the soldiers were at back of the wagon, but were unable to know if any had been hit.

'Spread out!' Frank shouted, 'and rush 'em!'

Brave words these, and for a few seconds it looked as though Frank's plan would work. It was he and Etta who led the men on one flank, while Lonny headed the others.

But before either group had gotten to within fifty yards of the wagon, the four carbeens opened up and began to take a terrible toll.

Etta heard the sickening thud of the bullet that struck Frank full in the chest and she turned and stared in a kind of angry grief as the big man crumpled and lay still at her feet.

She could see one of the soldiers now who had crept around and was firing from behind the dead horses. She raised her pistol and fired at the same time as Stredder pulled the trigger.

Etta's bullet grazed his cheek and the hammer of Stredder's carbeen clicked on a dud shell.

Stredder cursed roundly and managed to eject the shell and bring up a fresh one from the clip in the carbeen's stock.

'Goddam bitch!' Stredder swore, and forgot himself in the heat of that moment and took careful aim at the breast of the colourfully dressed girl.

Etta looked around her wildly. There were more men lying still or writhing on the ground than there were standing up. Her senses seemed a little blurred and the powder smoke drifted into her eyes and reeked in her nostrils.

What was happening? she wondered. Frank, Lonny and Lindquist were all down in this terrible, withering fire. Why had she escaped? Why, if not because she was a woman?

Her mouth drew down in a hard line as she sighted on the shoulder of a half-concealed trooper. She fired and saw the man jerk back and fall away.

She remembered the soldier who had been behind the dead horses, but she only had time to draw back the hammer of her gun before something hit her high on the shoulder, spinning her half round until she thought she must fall.

She heard a man's voice. *'Stredder! Leave her to me!'*

There was something oddly familiar about that voice despite the fact that it was pitched high with anger and fear. She heard two more of the gang scream and go down clutching their bellies, and from behind the bullet-shattered wagon a tall trooper emerged, carbeen to his shoulder.

Panic seized her, for she thought she had never been so close to death and any moment she expected to feel her breast shattered by leaden fire. But the man did not shoot and she turned, seeing the remainder of Frank's men fleeing for their lives and being dropped by the remorseless and terrible fire from that handful of troopers.

She could have dropped her gun and surrendered, but the thought never occurred to her. She turned and ran on shaking legs and felt pain in her side and in her shoulder and in her right thigh.

Somehow she got to her horse and somehow found the strength to mount and fall into the saddle. She rowelled the animal and headed out, only dimly aware that the firing had ceased.

She felt the warm, sticky blood oozing from the wounds and wondered how long she could last. What did it matter, anyway? Why she was even bothering to run?

She left the questions without attempting an answer, fighting hard to keep in the saddle and hold her pain-racked body erect. On and on she rode through an eternity of time. Her right leg was so stiff that she could hardly move her foot in the oxbow. Her shoulder was a smouldering flame of fire and the pain in her side grew worse.

Sometimes she almost lost consciousness and then her brain would clear for a while and, wondering greatly, she found herself still astride the game horse.

In her more lucid moments she tried to recognize the country, but completely failed to do so. Either through panic or by virtue of some obscure instinct the gelding was carrying her across arid stretches which she had never seen.

There were no farms here; no fields of waving corn; only desert and scrub land, and the bright cactus flowers were like splashes of blood on a green-grey and yellow land.

Time had long since ceased to exist for Etta Storm as she rode on, demanding the utmost from herself and the horse. She was once more semi-conscious when the gelding tripped and threw her from the saddle.

She rolled over and over and the thought came to her that this agony was like being stoned to death. Why was she still alive she could not understand as, slowly, she got to her feet, trembling and swaying and feeling the blood gush from her dust-choked mouth.

She heard the gelding's pitiful cries and, looking round, saw that both its forelegs were broken, the bones showing through the saline-flecked skin in several places. She half-walked, half-lurched across to where the horse lay, and his one visible eye looked at her imploringly.

Etta Storm had endured pain during her latter lifetime and now she was in agony, but she had never seen suffering such as this before and it was like a knife in her own breast.

She groped for her right-hand gun, but it was gone. The left-hand one had somehow remained in its holster and she drew it now and found that she had one load in the cylinder.

Carefully she aimed, standing close in so that there could be no possible mistake. The air quivered as the gun exploded and then silence came back and the gelding was out of pain.

Etta turned and walked, half-stumbling through a thicket of prickly pear. Beyond, as though in a dream, she saw a small Spanish Mission, built of white adobe.

Again she went forward and paused, panting, outside, and gazed into the cool, shadowed interior.

She wiped sweat and blood from her face and very slowly unbuckled her gun-belt, letting it fall to her feet.

She groped her way forward and now the thought in her mind became like an insistent hammering. *She must live for just a few more minutes: Please, God—*

Her right leg caused her to trip at the top step and she fell into the Mission and lay, panting and spent, in the semi-darkness.

Then she saw the altar steps and dragged herself along until she was lying sprawled upon them, her blood leaving its mark on the white-painted surface.

She lifted her head with a great effort and gazed at the exquisitely carved image of Mary and the infant Jesus.

'Mother of God,' she whispered, 'forgive me my sins afore I die ...'

And that was how Father Angelo found the unconscious, bullet-ridden girl.

At first everything around her was one vast and black ocean against which she fought with feeble strength. Sometimes the water engulfed her and she knew nothing and felt nothing.

Later, it was as though she hung suspended between earth and sky and faces floated towards her; kindly faces with gravely anxious eyes.

There was a priest whose expression was so full of peace that Etta no longer felt afraid. She knew he was a priest from the way he was dressed and the crucifix he always held in his hand. And there was a dark little man who whispered to her in Spanish and carried a black bag and seemed to be tending her in some way. And there was a plump woman—a Mexican—smiling and nodding, and there was the face of Dave Starr, and eventually their faces became less blurred and their voices were no longer mere whispers.

She opened her eyes and Dave Starr

was sitting by the bed, and she looked at him, studying his face for a long time, not daring to speak for fear everything would change and that darkness and pain would envelope her once more.

'Hallo, Etta. How you feelin'?'

The voice sounded strong and near and real for the first time and she roused herself, moving her limbs and feeling only slight pain.

'Dave,' she whispered. 'Is it true? That I'm alive, I mean.'

He nodded. 'Not only alive, Etta, but you're goin' to be fine in a little while. But you've given us some anxious times.'

'How—how long have I bin here, wherever it is?'

'Six weeks!'

Her eyes opened wide for the first time. 'You're joshin' me!'

He shook his head. 'It's true. You've bin delirious off an' on for quite a spell—'

'I remember seein' a priest an' a little dark man, a Mex, I guess—'

'Sure. He's the village doctor who got the bullets out and saved your life. But it

296

was Father Angelo, the priest, who found you in his Mission, the church belongin' to his community here in Santa Donna—'

A dark cloud passed over the girl's pale face. 'Why—why have you-all done this? I ain't fit to be saved, you know that, Dave. You know I robbed an' killed! Why didn't you just leave me to die—?'

'Take it easy; don't go gettin' yourself all excited. There's a lot've things you don't know yet, Etta. Fact o' the matter is, you ain't killed anyone, though you tried some! As for the robberies, well, the men responsible 've mostly paid—'

'You mean the Sutters are dead, don't you?'

'Frank an' Lonny are dead; so's Doc Dufresne an' Lindquist an' a couple others. The rest are in custody.'

'You *are* a lawman, Dave; ain't that so?'

He nodded. 'Right now, you gotta go back to sleep an' I'll tell you the rest of the story later ...'

By the end of that week, Etta was able to go out for the first time and walk as far as the *plaza* with the aid of a stick and Dave's strong arm.

They sat in the shade of an ancient walnut tree and he described how Sutter's gang had been broken and most of the stolen money recovered. Henry Forrest was well on the road to recovery and had sworn that the slim masked rider, now known to be Etta Storm, had fired only at him. Coles and the other Express men had been killed by carbeen shells at the hands of Sutter and his men.

The dark cloud had passed from Etta's face, leaving it lovelier than ever in its calm tranquility.

'This town, Dave. Santa Donna; it's—'

'You like it, don't you?'

She nodded. 'Better'n any place I've ever known. I—I reckon I'll stay here, Dave. Mebbe I can find some job. I don't care what it is, just so long as it's clean an' honest—'

Dave stood up. 'You feel like walkin' to the Mission?' He took her arm and together they made their slow way, with Etta limping and using her stick.

They stood on the steps outside and he held her gently and said: 'This is where we'll be married, Etta—'

'No! You cain't, Dave! I told you! What difference does it make if I didn't fire the actual shots as killed those men? I was ready to kill an' steal an' likely I'll be arrested just as soon as—'

But from the shadows inside the church, Father Angelo appeared and his gaze rested on Etta's face with a deep and compassionate understanding.

'Do not deny the miracle that has happened, my child. You came back from the dead and are now re-born. Do not cling to a guilt which no longer exists. God in His great mercy has forgiven you. Do you, therefore, forgive yourself and accept the love that this man offers you.'

Then Father Angelo was gone and for a long while they stood there, and at length Etta's hand reached out and clasped Dave's and in her velvet blue eyes lay an expression of unutterable peace ...

The publishers hope that this book has given you enjoyable reading. Large Print Books are especially designed to be as easy to see and hold as possible. If you wish a complete list of our books, please ask at your local library or write directly to: Dales Large Print Books, Long Preston, North Yorkshire, BD23 4ND, England.

This Large Print Book for the Partially sighted, who cannot read normal print, is published under the auspices of

THE ULVERSCROFT FOUNDATION